The Book of Gems

ALSO BY FRAN WILDE

THE GEM UNIVERSE SERIES
The Jewel and Her Lapidary
The Fire Opal Mechanism

THE BONE UNIVERSE SERIES
Updraft
Cloudbound
Horizon

THE BOOK OF GEMS

FRAN WILDE

TOR PUBLISHING GROUP
NEW YORK

THE BOOK OF GEMS

Cover art by Tommy Arnold
Cover design by Christine Foltzer

A Tordotcom Book
Published by Tor Publishing Group / Tom Doherty Associates
120 Broadway
New York, NY 10271

www.tor.com

Tor* is a registered trademark of Macmillan Publishing Group, LLC.

ISBN 978-1-250-19655-2 (ebook)
ISBN 978-1-250-19656-9 (trade paperback)

First Edition: 2023

For Iris, Meg, Raq, both Elises, and everyone who sees magic in science, science in magic, and both in art.

PART ONE

*Dr. Devina Brunai, gem-anthropologist, Netherby
Laboratory and Manufacturing
To Chairwoman Constance Yance, Society for Scientific
Endeavors of the Six Republics*

Dear Honored Chairwoman Yance,

For the past three months, our laboratory has received no word from our director, Dr. Aleric Netherby. His last messages from his research trip to the Jeweled Valley, funded by the Society, were troubling to say the least. If the Society has knowledge of him that would help the laboratory appease our clients and creditors, we would be grateful.

In exchange, I offer what information we have, enclosing a sample of those final messages. If Dr. Netherby has, as I believe, disappeared, I further offer to travel to the Jeweled Valley in order to ensure he and his research are preserved. Yes, I did apply for the Society travel grant he received, and yes, we were seen fighting on the day of his departure, but I returned to work in his laboratory during his absence, as agreed, and have been a model of support ever since, continuing to deliver escritoire gems and mechanisms to our clients, including the

Society. I hope this is sufficient evidence to reassure the Society that I wish only the best for our esteemed colleague.

If the Society grants me leave to travel, I propose to complete Netherby's work if he is unable to do so. If I can discover what has happened to the doctor, or the cause for his increasingly strange messages, I would be honored to transmit that knowledge to you. I understand that, at present, the valley is far more dangerous than usual, and that passage within its borders is still heavily restricted. I will take all due precautions against the ongoing geological instability.

I hope the Society will assist me with my passage.

Dr. Devina Brunai, assistant to Dr. Aleric Netherby

~

NEWTOWN, IRONFORD REPUBLIC, ANN. ___15.

From Chairwoman Constance Yance, Society for
Scientific Endeavors of the Six Republics
To Dr. Devina Brunai, Netherby Laboratory and
Manufacturing

Madame, while I am grateful for the information you've shared, I cannot support your request for funds. You may not travel to the Jeweled Valley.

Yours,
Dr. Constance Yance

1.

DEV BOARDED THE TWO-CARRIAGE train at Ironford Station well before dawn. A pale young woman with damp brown hair and no cloak, she glanced over her shoulder repeatedly before climbing into the carriage.

Once on board, Dev pressed her cheek against the window frame and eyed the shivering porter as he loaded a single bag of mail and two crates of supplies into the other carriage. The young scientist stared without blinking, even after the porter waved a blue handkerchief engineward.

Dev watched the platform with the same intensity that had always unnerved her colleagues. "You won't make that stone talk to you by staring it down." They'd laughed at her in school. "You can't scare a gem, Devina," even Netherby had teased. "No matter how fierce you seem." But now, she stared as if she could scare off any remaining threats to her journey. When the sun cracked the horizon, illuminating the tracks and the station in golden light, she squinted and kept staring until the train jolted forward.

Not until Newtown's walls began to recede and the train slowly began to accelerate did she look away. Soon, the first of four far-flung bridges that marked the edge of Ironford and the only access to the Jeweled Valley whipped past. Only when the train passed through a mountain tunnel and crossed the next six-span bridge and the brittle Cutter River below did her fear that someone might drag her from her seat ease.

Neither the embossed leather envelope containing her forged letter of introduction to the valley and the archeological dig, nor the Esteemed Scientist's notes and communications, nor the weight of the experimentally modified micrograph in its elegant case on her lap that she had removed from Netherby's laboratory without permission— none of it made Dev feel like she'd successfully embarked on her mission to find her mentor as much as the train's rumble across the bridge, and the wide gap of distance it implied.

And although she'd nicked the micrograph, which, with the case opened, resembled quite exactly those machines advertised in Netherby Labs catalogs as a *harmonium-enhanced crystal-verification tool for the most discerning of lab-grown gem owners,* Dev was confident she hadn't made any other mistakes. She would keep the machine hidden. Her letter to the Society had been carefully worded and had gained her a quicker reply than she'd expected. Yance was so outraged by Dev's request that she'd even signed the escritoire transmission. Which Dev then easily transferred to the forged letter. She'd burned a quarter of her savings on the next ticket to the valley, informed her colleagues she was feeling ill, and before anyone in the lab, or the Society, knew better, gathered up her small bag of tools, two sandwiches, and a small box of chocolate, and headed for the station.

Dev rubbed the crick in her neck with soldering-calloused fingers and touched the shard pendant at her throat. "Now, we'll see," she whispered, and turned toward the contents of her satchel. She lifted out the micrograph and eyed its polished rosewood and enamel case.

"Tickets!" The conductor's distant call startled her, and the wooden micrograph case nearly tumbled to the carriage floor. Dev wedged the instrument, the size of two sharp-cornered fists, securely between her skirts and the hard bench on which she sat and pressed her hands against the leather satchel until her pulse calmed.

"You are a scientist on Society business. Panic is not conducive to scientific thought," she whispered to herself sternly. Years of study under the strictest instructors the academies of the Far Reaches had to offer had taught Dev that data calmed her nerves, even if the end results were not always what she expected. Years of subsequent work under the Society's watchful eye had further taught her to be cautious about which questions she asked, and to cover her tracks as much as possible. And the past few months, working under Netherby's increasingly concerning restrictions, had taught her to plan ahead.

Because she surely needed data, before she fell into the same kind of trouble Netherby was so obviously in. His last messages had been so strange. He'd managed to transmit a map, even. One with ancient scripts in the margins. Odd demands.

Dev was certain that when she found him, she'd finally gain acceptance to the Society herself, no matter how outrageous Constance Yance considered her theories on the Book of Gems.

It is real. All of it.

Dev would find proof she was right. She already had proof. Well, she used to. It was stolen from her. By Netherby.

"If you had sent me to the valley in the first place," Dev murmured to the paint peeling off the carriage's ceiling, "none of this would have happened."

The train clattered along the tracks in staccato reply, and the conductor worked his way toward her quickly. There were only a few other people on the train, and none in Dev's car.

When he reached her, he smiled encouragingly. "How long do you stay?"

She handed him her ticket, the thin paper transparent in the dim lighting. "In the valley? A week at most." Anything longer and her colleagues would get suspicious. Worse, she'd miss the Symposium—the Society's quadrennial review of all research related to gemology. And this year, the Symposium was finally including a study on the Book of Gems. Netherby was the featured guest speaker. Dev had timed her own expedition to correlate with a triumphant return just prior to the event.

"Miss?"

Dev had sunk so deep into her thoughts that she barely heard the conductor. "Doctor," she muttered automatically, making sure the micrograph remained out of sight.

"Doctor, then." The conductor's voice had a deep valley twang. "You're heading to the dig? Seems like the only reason folks from Ironford travel all the way out here."

"Yes, sir." Dev knew her manners, thanks to her grandmother. Don't pry. Don't be too forward.

"And you'll be staying where?" The conductor could pry, as he was likely about to check her credentials anyway.

"At the Deaf King Inn." At least, she hoped so. Her grandmother's cousins had run the inn for generations. There was nowhere else for outsiders to stay in the valley. If they had no vacancy she'd be out of luck before she even began.

To her relief, the man nodded. "Last Ironford scientist was much less polite." The conductor leaned on the back of Dev's worn wooden bench as if he intended to stay and chat for the rest of the journey. "Quite something, that one. Ordered everyone in the train around, or tried to."

She was being quizzed. Dev smiled sadly, deciding honesty was best. Or some honesty, at least. "My mentor. Netherby."

"Ah. The Society's papered the trains with his Symposium pamphlets." The conductor pulled a crumpled flyer from his vest. It was decorated with key words from Netherby's research and carefully edited messages: *Be the first among the Republics to see!* "Your Society finds all sorts of ways to profit from our dig, doesn't it?" He raised both eyebrows.

Dev was about to agree but then cleared her throat, remembering who she was supposed to be working for. "Of course not. The dig belongs to the valley. The Society is only here to help. To provide tools, methods . . ."

The man chuckled. "That's what everyone says. But even your Netherby's eyes glittered when he said it."

"When did you last speak to him?" Back home, everyone was waiting on Netherby's next transmission. They described his upcoming Symposium presentation as if it was already historic and earth-shattering. But here in the valley, they'd apparently seen right through him. Or he'd let himself be seen.

"Oh, weeks ago. We hoped he'd gone home. But now

you're here . . ." The man's eyebrows rose higher. Dev half smiled.

"Here I am. Just trying to find out what happened. Then I'll go home too." She said it as hopefully as she could muster. If Netherby had left the valley, and the dig, no one in Ironford was aware of it. She needed to find out more.

Dev took a calming breath and waited for more questions. The train climbed higher into the hills, its speed pressing her into her seat. The conductor braced himself at a switchback, one hand on the seat. When the route finally smoothed the conductor coughed softly. "You have your Society's letter, then, Doctor? To give to the dig master?"

Dev had one, yes. She made a show of rooting carefully in her bag for the thick envelope with the Society's seal on it, avoiding any motions that would reveal the stolen micrograph. A conductor this talkative would surely take note of it, and might tell others in turn. The train rocked to one side and then the other as it went around another bend.

The conductor didn't smile back when she handed the letter to him. He read the letter, then began to put it in his pocket.

"Won't I need that for the dig?" Dev asked, alarmed. She didn't want to relinquish the document. Didn't want to lose her chance, even if Netherby had already squandered it.

"I'll let them know. You have one week's time in the valley," the conductor said. He handed her a small silver disk inscribed with basket-weave edge work. The weaving tendrilled out and through a single word: *visitor,* binding it to the center of the seal. As Dev ran her thumb over the cold, textured disk, the conductor walked away with her forged letter. To pursue him would risk getting thrown out of the valley before she even entered. The seal felt cold and heavy in her fingers. She tucked it away inside her canvas lab coat—the only coat she owned.

"Blast you, Netherby," she whispered. She watched the conductor pass between the cars. He settled onto his own bench near the engine, lying down until all Dev could see were his mud-caked boots. When she was sure he was committed to a long, if uncomfortable, nap, Dev turned once again to the micrograph and her pendant.

The jagged, wire-wrapped stone hung from a tarnished chain around her neck, all she had left of her research, and her inheritance. She unclasped the necklace, carefully running her thumb over the small shard of lapis lazuli it contained. A single curl of gold traced the broken edge, the last remaining part of an inscription. It belonged to a full page that Dev's grandmother had given her. Before she died, the old woman told Dev that she believed the page had fallen from the original Book of Gems. She'd clutched Dev's hand, willing her to believe too, that this page was different than all the commonly available fakes. Dev, loving her very much, had promised to protect the legacy.

Now, with a pair of needle-nosed pliers, Dev began carefully extracting the shard from the pendant's bezel.

When she first came to work for Netherby, he'd rarely taken the legends about the Book of Gems seriously, nor those of the valley. He was too focused on making the synthetic gems that drove the Society's communications tools—the escritoires—and powered his own machines. He made the best artificial gems in the Six Republics. They'd made him rich and had paid for the lab. To him, the Book of Gems was something everyone kept a copy of, out of superstition. Sometimes he used his lab copy—a replica made of Society imitation lapis—to inspire his own gem designs. But it mostly served as a paperweight.

The lab copy certainly *looked* like Dev's grandmother's page. But lab-grown lapis was easy to make. The original Book of Gems, hand etched and inked centuries before the Seven Kingdoms had become Six Republics, was rumored to have been lost when the ruined palace of the Valley Jewels was swallowed by the earth.

"Besides," Netherby laughed when Dev tried to tell him that her thin blue plate of lapis was much older than the copies, "the original book's supposed to turn outsiders' eyes to diamonds if they read it, and their tongues to moonstone if they speak the words. And neither have happened to you."

Dev was determined to prove him wrong.

"That will cost you, Devina," she said, mimicking his nasally voice as she worked on the shard, prizing away each section of the silver bezel without breaking it. She'd need that again.

Netherby had turned her wish to use his equipment for her research into a way to enrich his own. In order to pay for bench time after hours, and with Netherby turning a blind eye to Society rules, she'd saved every penny. A shared room at the cheapest Newtown boardinghouse, carefully laundering her only lab coat in the sink each night, and patching her cheap boots herself had allowed Dev to afford her research. It earned her awkward looks from her colleagues, and insults from Netherby, but she'd had no other choice, so she grew accustomed to it all.

Even before Netherby filed for the same Society grant she'd sought, Dev's situation had grown worse. After he witnessed her first micrograph experiments, it became his lifetime goal to "find the remains of the original Book of Gems, and the source of its mutative powers." Sure enough, the Society determined that Netherby—and not Dev—would go to the valley, see the ancient palace excavation, and attempt to secure the original Book of Gems before anyone else did. And he forbade her from doing more experiments in the lab in his absence.

All this had been her fault, of course. She'd been so desperate for any opportunity to assess the page that she'd let him read the printout from the first micrograph assay. She'd been hoping he'd support her eventual paper. Or put her forward for Society approval—things that her university professors in the Far Reaches had steadfastly refused unless she let her obsession with the book and its pages go.

"Possession of a valley artifact outside the walls of the Society? That will get you in dire trouble, Devina," she muttered. She finished taking apart the bezel and held the bare shard in her hand. She put her tools back in her bag, and the bezel with them. Frustration soured her tongue as she recalled Netherby's clammy fingers on the lapis page, the writing revealed by the micrograph starting to fade before she could read all of it, and his too-smooth voice telling the entire lab she was not to be trusted to do any further experiments on the premises, only production work. Much more quietly, Netherby said he would help Dev gain admission to the Society if she agreed to stay under these conditions.

When she'd hesitated, he lifted the page high, smashed it against her workbench, and scooped the pieces into his pocket.

Then, she obeyed. She hated herself for that. So much so that she never dared to test the small lapis shard she'd found wedged beneath her lab bench. She set the piece in a simple bezel and wore it every day to remind herself of her failings, and her goal. But when it became obvious that he might not return, Dev grew braver.

The clatter of train wheels against track echoed the beat of the promises she'd made to him, to the Society, to herself, each demanding her attention: *complete his work... return that knowledge to the Society*.

Dev massaged her jaw; she'd been grinding her teeth, thinking again about the duplicity of those words. In the first draft of her letter, she'd written and crossed out her intent to toss Netherby's bones deep into the valley's newly opened crevasses. Maybe that would have worked better. But many on the Society's funding committee still counted Dr. Aleric Netherby as a friend, including Chairwoman Yance. Dev needed their goodwill. Or at least their forbearance.

She hadn't gotten either. All she'd gained, she'd done for herself. And now, she had a few unobserved hours where she could finally collect more data. No prying colleagues. No judgmental rules of the Society saying what was proper science and what wasn't. No restrictions. Once she reached the valley, Dev knew she'd be out of opportunities. She had to do her experiments now, on the rocking train, with one eye out in case someone passed through the car.

She touched a finger lightly to the micrograph case and

looked over the high-backed seat toward the carriage door. *Was* she being watched? Two passengers sat in the other compartment, but they were deeply engaged with a basket of food. Dev's fingers itched to open the micrograph, to try once more to make the lapis shard reveal its secrets. Because that's what had happened the first time, in the lab.

That first time, she'd gasped at the results that poured from the machine's side—a crystal structure that looked more like music than science. She hoped she had enough of the page to reproduce even a portion of the results now. She longed to see again the impossibly complex structures that appeared on the page after the experiment with the definitive traces of ruby in the deep-cut inscriptions. More important, she hoped to regain proof that the lab's micrograph had managed to unveil the presence of structures known only to gems from the valley itself. *It was real.*

Better than that. Before the micrograph, the page had been blank. Afterward, it revealed ornate script: a standard injunction to the lapidaries—all she could read before the page was shattered, and before Netherby bore most of it away: *A lapidary must obey the gems.* Perhaps her page had described gem handling, long ago. The micrograph must have shaken loose embedded minerals. However, what had gained Netherby's notice most was that this injunction was in ancient valley script—something her grandmother had taught her to read—not standard Republic script.

~

Netherby always claimed the ability to make gems "as good as the Jeweled Valley's," but in the case of the lapis page, he could not reproduce it. And he wouldn't let Dev try. Worse, when he departed for the valley, Netherby repeated his warnings, keeping Dev away from more illicit experiments, saying, "If you don't behave, I'll ruin your career and your Society application. Keep the lab running." And she'd agreed. But she had her own secrets too.

Now she regarded the shard, remembering glittering ink scrawling across the lapis surface: *A lapidary must obey*—

An illicit experiment on the train might produce the first clue as to Netherby's fate, and thus the whereabouts of everything the Esteemed Scientist had stolen from her. She wanted that data back. But could she risk it?

The train neared another bridge. A third of the way through the journey. She would run out of time to safely use the micrograph if she didn't start now. She shifted the micrograph to her lap. When the train sounded its high-pitched whistle, she jumped again. Perhaps it was better to wait until she was settled in the valley, rather than never arriving at all.

If her grandmother's cousins let her stay at the Deaf King, that is. She didn't have nearly enough money to pay the fees. Valley lodgings came at a high cost to visitors. Understandable, given how much the Society had extracted from the area. Dev grimaced.

But if it was discovered that she'd smuggled a tool capable of mapping and copying the crystal structure of any gem with her into the valley, she would be tossed into the nearest crevasse herself. The Jeweled Valley's laws and the Society's rules on such things were absolute. Better do it now.

Netherby had designed the original micrographs to analyze the chemical and physical structure of lab gems for flaws.

But, once Dev recalibrated it to analyze her grandmother's page, the machine became capable of so much more. She couldn't leave it behind.

The train's click-clack rhythm seemed to mock the time Dev had wasted working dutifully on Netherby's escritoires and lab-created gems, the echoed words from his last messages in that ancient script running the margins: . . . *time lost time lost time.*

Dev felt a cold current run across the back of her neck. Lost time, *indeed.* Over the course of the past four months, she'd convinced herself that Netherby had been right: that helping him would get her name back on the paper he'd submitted without her and win her Society acceptance. *A Treatise on the Structural Composition of Valley Minerals and True Source of the Book of Gems*—he'd even kept her title! At the time, that had seemed hopeful to her. She'd resolved to wait, all while Netherby used *her* work to get Society funding to go to the dig.

Netherby's strange disappearance had given Dev an opportunity. *No more waiting.*

. . . *I promise to complete his great work.* Yes, Dev would do that now.

She would finish the research. Immediately, and without anyone else's interference.

Carefully, she lifted the micrograph's lid, braced it between her satchel and her thigh, and placed her shard within. The micrograph contained a mercury-balanced, lab-grown harmonium gem of Netherby's own design, very heavy for its size. The stone's resonances marked differences between production lots, initially. Now, with Dev's adjustments, it traced the crystal structures of anything placed within.

Dev's lapis shard settled deep in the mechanism.

Her hands shook with the train's motions. One more bridge, and then she couldn't risk any more work.

After glancing to be sure that the door to the other carriage remained closed, Dev flipped the micrograph's tiny switch. The mechanism vibrated the mercury, and a crystalline structure report began to spool from its side on a thin strip of gem-imprinted paper. The seams of the micrograph glowed bright blue in the predawn dark.

Dev hid the glow beneath her lab coat and pressed on.

The micrograph—and the lapis shard inside—began to hum.

Dev covered her ears, groaning as the noise crept from the micrograph and into her bones. This hadn't happened before. The machine began to grow hot and curls of smoke started to emerge from the case. Dev panicked. She reached a trembling hand to the micrograph and fumbled with the switch. It stuck fast in the "on" position, until, finally, her fingers pressed hard enough to toggle it off. That provided only marginal relief. The glow disappeared, the smoke dissipated, but the humming didn't stop!

The sound almost had words to it. Syllables with no sense. Dev's mind spun trying to attach meaning to the hum, while simultaneously trying to hide the machine away before the conductor noticed the disturbance.

No motion from the other carriages . . . *yet*.

Carefully, wincing the whole time from the hum's echoes, Dev reached inside the micrograph for the lapis shard—which was hot against her fingers. She reached in her satchel for a pair of gloves and slid them on. As gently as possible, she wrapped the bezel around the stone again. Only then did the sound stop. Dev tucked all her supplies back in her satchel, secured the micrograph, then laid her head on the back of the seat in front of her. She closed her eyes to ease the waves of dizziness crashing over her, all the while holding tight to the shard.

2

"LURAI, I NEED SOMEONE TO go to the market for me. The pantry's nearly bare. And Calia, hurry and straighten the guest rooms before school; be a dear and help your sister." The older woman's voice held a note of tension in it. Breakfast service was over, but that meant lunch and dinner preparations were beginning.

Lurai sighed. "Gran, I can see to it." Calia would do the rooms too fast. Her sister had swept the breakfast tables, more or less, but a dirty spoon and a mug still sat on the table nearest the fire. The Deaf King's kitchen had been stretched thin for so long—even now, Gran was making today's pies out of last night's leftovers. Lurai had considered putting "Bare Pantry" on the menu and charging for it. The errand could wait until Lurai had time to go. Plus, the market was near the dig, and Lurai needed to stop by again, to see if they had any news.

"Don't you even think of stopping at the dig. Lannert will bring word if they find anything. Don't pester the man." Gran seemed to read her mind. Lurai bet she probably could.

"If we could only know what happened. If I could find them—" she started, but Gran grasped her upper arm hard.

"Ow!"

"The only thing you'll find at that dig is trouble, same as your mother. I couldn't bear to lose you both. Promise me, Lurai." Gran Idary's grip was as tight as a ward wrapping. "No going in the fortress."

Dev bent her head. "I promise," she mumbled.

Gran shook her arm. "For real."

"I will obey the gems and the book, and all who have come before me." She recited the oldest vow in the valley from memory until Gran looked satisfied.

"Good. We won't have any more among us disappear then. Now figure out how to talk the market into giving us vegetables on credit." Gran turned back to the oven, blinking back sadness.

They'd already run credit with the vegetable sellers this month, Lurai knew. Maybe Gran thought she was magic and could conjure goodwill from a stone. *Well, I have kept the place running since Mum vanished; that's pretty magic,* Lurai thought. Another day of poached fowl from the river wouldn't be too bad for business. *Besides, where else would business go? The Deaf King is the only place for visitors in the valley.*

Lurai rubbed at her temples with silver-wrapped fingers before carrying the rest of the dishes to the kitchen. Since the quakes began in earnest, and Mum had gone, the ringing in her ears troubled her more and more. She pinched the wires wrapping her earlobes, trying to relieve the tension. Once, she'd hoped to make something of the inn, a real historic holiday place for valley tourists. Now, she just wanted to keep enough money coming in to pay the bills.

Taking care of her family—her gran and her sister in particular—was Lurai's goal now.

"Time for school, Calia!" she called, her voice sounding more like Gran's every day.

The girl was only three years younger, but Lurai would make sure she had a good life. Calia's boots thumped the stairs. The door slammed as she called a cheery good-bye.

Beneath those noises and the usual din of her gran humming a valley song as she cooked, Lurai heard the *tick-tick-tick* of the inn's ancient escritoire. The machine, buried under a pile of handwritten bills on the inn manager's desk, shook as if possessed.

"What *now*," Lurai groaned. That escritoire, a gift to her mother from one of the Society scholars, only ever brought bad news.

Except today, when the gem-printed paper read, in Lapidarian, *New guest en route, evening train. Society visitor. Ironford.*

The message was unsigned, but Lurai guessed at the sender. Lapidarian meant someone from the valley for sure. And the conductor was sweet on Gran.

"Best make more pies!" she called. "Another scholar coming." And past time to get to the market. And perhaps the dig.

It would be good to have another guest who could afford to pay the fees. Lurai shoved the printout on top of the bills and grabbed a basket and her coat.

3.

DEV MUST HAVE SLEPT, because she woke to the sun pressing through the carriage's windows, directly into her eyes. Her head throbbed. Glancing down, she saw the writing on the lapis shard had changed to read *A prince must—*

Prince? There were no princes in the Jeweled Valley that she knew of. If she found the opportunity, perhaps she could ask someone at the dig or the inn, politely, about local legends. As daylight strobed between the thin trunks of the quickly passing mountain evergreens, Dev blinked at the lapis shard until the train neared the last bridge, then quickly restrung it around her neck.

~

JEWELED VALLEY, ANN. ___14.

Netherby to lab: Have arrived. Valley officials accepted my credentials. Arranged lodging at the Deaf King Inn. Shoddy accommodations. Found guide to take me to the excavation tomorrow. Others are already here. Drs. Sen and Oen convey their regards to Dev.

~

JEWELED VALLEY, ANN. ___14.

Netherby to lab: The Society's management of the dig is somewhat porous, so I will send back samples and rubbings from artifacts. I have inscribed a map of the site. More of the book is rumored to be in the dig, but so far, we fight over crumbs. One hundred fifteen original gems. Only seventeen survived the Fall of the Jewels, but have since been reduced to three—SAVE ME—perhaps four, while only scraps of cheap chatoyant jasper are being given to science. Meantime, the dig master, a valley man named Lannert, refuses to allow us broad access. Only valley workers may enter the dig. They have gathered several gem shards, but will not share them with outsiders. Very frustrating. Which of these are pieces of the lost gems, destroyed during the fall of the kingdom? Which are new gems, created in the belly of the valley? Could any be the [indecipherable], the Inveterate Diamond, the Truth Sapphire? The Ruby Cabochon—MY BLOOD MY BREATH— I know it must be here. In all cases, finding more gems to power the Society's research OR THE TRUTH—the original book, or the gems themselves, FIND THE THRONE AND [unintelligible], must happen soon. As I work, the dig seems to whisper its own stories. I am not imagining it. My head aches with it. I am becoming unbound by it. Dev, be sure to promptly deliver the next set of gems to our clients.

~

One more bridge before the train reached the valley. Dev had been on board for hours, without breakfast or lunch. *That must have been the cause of my dizzy spell,* she thought.

Food. She needed to eat. *That will help.*

Dev caught a glance at herself in the glass window of the train car as she unwrapped a sandwich. Her hair rose like a rooster's tail on the side where she'd slept. Her fingers were stained with gem-dust ink from the micrograph printout. She did not, in fact, look or feel at all like someone traveling on behalf of the Society for Scientific Endeavors of the Six Republics.

She hurried to repair her appearance before they arrived. If she was to successfully fly beneath the notice of the Society, she had to look like she was from the Society. Constance Yance could never hear of a disheveled scientist's arrival at the dig.

She glanced at the sketched portrait of Yance on the flyer the conductor had left behind: high-piled hair coifed in the latest heavily curled style, a deep blue Society cloak pinned at the neck with a lab-created gem. Her eyes bright—they had been hand-tinted blue on the flier—as if looking straight into Dev's soul.

Dev swallowed hard, then calmed her nerves by checking the contents of her bag—sandwich, chocolate, medical kit, lab tools, a change of practical, dark-hued clothes for archeological work, and, of course, an experimental micrograph safely tucked away. *Good.*

She gingerly touched the machine, as if it might begin to speak. It stayed silent.

Dev ran her fingers over the machine's case. She'd had such strange dreams. Her fingers discovered a report spooled in a corner of the satchel, its ink-printed paper as smooth as the lapis shard had once been.

She withdrew it, remembering more of what she'd done. Illicit research. Without Society approval. On a train, in fact! Averting her gaze from Yance's portrait, Dev decided that she would review the report data while she ate.

The conductor remained in the other car as the train crossed the last bridge. The bridge spans glittered with inset gem fragments and metal embellishments. Wards, Dev knew. Superstition. Against what? Outsiders, likely. Or gravity. A drop to the river far below would definitely be fatal.

So much of the Six Republics' history, its wars and alliances, was built on the belief in the valley's powerful gems. So much time had been spent—Dev's included—mimicking certain elements of gems' powers, then placing them in objects and selling them. You couldn't throw a rock without hitting someone who *supposedly* had valley family who might like to make something gem-powered for you. It had gotten so bad, Dev refused to speak of her own family's origins. Few would treat her like a scientist if they knew, Netherby being a prime example. And now she was headed back there, hoping her distant cousins would help her. Even though she knew they would hate the work she did, and the loss of the lapis page her grandmother had entrusted to her.

Ambition, Dev cursed inwardly. *I've wasted my inheritance on ambition. And I'll likely do it again. I have to know the truth.*

While Dev munched on the simple sandwich she'd assembled in the early hours before the train, her mind wandered. Was it possible that the book had some power that hadn't been discovered during all the research the Society had poured into the valley gems? Dev believed so. Now she suspected Netherby's strange behavior and disappearance was tied to the same phenomenon.

And she was determined to prove it, if she could avoid trouble while she was here.

Not until she saw the two local citizens disembark at the first stop in the valley, the small village that was now host to the large archeological dig, did Dev spread the micrograph report across her lap. The train still had a slow climb up the next mountain to where the Deaf King Inn kept lookout over the valley, but, with the exception of the conductor, she was now nearly alone.

The data was deeply complex, even to Dev's experienced eye. The results looked like sound recordings, not crystal-graphs. Her previous assay on the lapis page had displayed something similar, she thought. But Netherby had taken those results with him too.

What if I've misremembered?

Before the train reached its final stop, Dev made a few notes in the margins of the report, marking different points in the data that seemed more manageable: A peak here. A dip there. She couldn't understand how one lapis shard could generate so much data. And a few lines that looked like valley script on the printout—no. That was impossible.

Her head throbbed, as it had on and off since the early afternoon.

Unable to focus through her headache and the heaving motion of the train any longer, Dev tucked the new data away in a leather folio, together with Netherby's correspondence.

Just seeing the contents of the folder made her head pound more. The lab had received copies of most of

Netherby's escritoire correspondence with the Society. Everything, from his frequent requests for more funds, to his gossip about the locals, to his later increasingly confused and panicked messages. Dev had taken it all from the lab that morning. Among the transcripts, she found her own reports: crystallograms, careful notes about frequency and amplification. The original lapis page analysis. And the SAVE ME message from the lab.

The presence of her own research in the folder felt like a scalpel prying at her temples. She fought to center herself. Where Dev had circled numbers, Netherby's scrawl had overruled them, highlighting a new pattern on the original scans. He'd used his pen to outline a vague silhouette of the valley itself, based on what he wanted the information to be, not what it was. Seeing his "research," Dev bit her cheek. Then she came to her own neat handwriting: *Evidence of elevated harmonics, comparable to the escritoire gems. Nothing dangerous. D.B.* She'd signed that one.

The Society had known it was her work then. And they'd sent Netherby anyway and denied Dev.

~

LABORATORY NOTES, ANN. ___14:

Dr. Devina Brunai to Dr. Aleric Netherby

Lapis contains unknown gem interstitials. A micrograph analysis produced evidence of complex structures known only to authenticated valley gems. A deeper examination us-ing sonic and crystallogram assays generated feedback that seemed to sing before the page shattered. I can't explain this scientifically, so I'll remove it later.

Within the data, there is a shadow, hinting at more data, that I cannot yet understand.

It is not magic. These are just chemical and crystal structures, not magic.

I'll know more when I can get more samples. Please request from the Society.

4.

Netherby to the Society: I have arrived at the easternmost point of the valley's newly opened crevasse. The dig here is guarded at all times. All who work at the dig seem extremely superstitious. I expect it is the trauma caused by the quakes, but it is strange behavior: they repeat ancient phrases before entering; they wrap fingers, arms, ears, and even their feet with silver wire. They do not trust anyone they do not know. There may be difficult, expensive times ahead. Only the innkeeper and her daughter, my erstwhile guides, seem amenable.

~

Dev disembarked from the carriage, her head still pounding. The tracks terminated abruptly in a quickly constructed roundabout, just beyond a small wooden shelter painted red and blue at the edge of a steep cliff. She peered over the edge and saw the remains of a toppled bridge far below. It had been a difficult ride. The final bridge had swayed in the wind and beneath the train's weight and a tunnel had to be cleared in order to allow the engine through. This especially gave her a bad feeling about her ability to return quickly to Ironford, or even the village below, if she needed to. The whole hillside looked precarious.

She wondered if she should get back on the train.

But the engineer, who'd slowly taken the train around the loop, waved and pointed to the signpost, calling, "Inn's that way!" over the hum of the engine. He quickly set off back down the mountain before Dev could reply.

It was growing dark, and Dev watched the shining train disappear into the mountains, leaving her alone.

Her patched boots crunched the rough gravel path from the station to a barely paved trailhead. A faded marker pointing away from the ravine read THE DEAF KING INN in barely visible paint. Likely built far from the town. On purpose, Dev realized. To keep the visitors away from the locals. And now from the dig as well.

A second, newer sign, just below the first, read *Visitors: All must report to valley officials, declare all goods, and date of departure.* Well, she'd done that. Hopefully a conductor counted.

No valley materials will be permitted to leave the area, stiff penalties apply. Dev resisted pressing a hand over her pendant. The sign could not see what she wore.

What makes you believe you are the only one who can find Netherby when the Society cannot? She stared at the trees.

"I know how he thinks," she reminded herself. *Better than the Society does.*

With the Symposium looming, the Society would be desperate for any news. No matter how hard they tried to deny her, Dev was certain that returning with proof of the book's existence would put the Society in her debt. She would get to the bottom of this. But first, she needed to find Netherby's bags. And have a long sleep.

Netherby, when he departed four months ago, had done so with all the pomp and expensive equipment that marked any great Society-sponsored undertaking. She recalled Netherby's canvas bags, with his gold-lettered initials on them. The pneumatic jack and first aid kits that the Society had loaded onto the train carriage, the whole laboratory watching the grand send-off. She remembered Constance Yance's words to the gathered press: "We hope Dr. Netherby's endeavors will pay off as handsomely as his ongoing work with gem-communications!" But there had been no such windfall yet. The Society must be out substantial sums, Dev suspected. With hungry creditors circling the Society, Netherby's absence must be causing Yance discomfort too. But not yet enough to support Dev's journey.

Eventually, Dev would prove herself a hero for finding Netherby. "And I'm going to do more than that," Dev announced to the trees. She began walking, her satchel strap already digging into her shoulder.

After what felt like an hour of painful walking, Dev gasped. Beyond the trees stood an ancient inn, which clearly had once been painted bright colors, although those had faded to gray and brown. A porch held rocking chairs trimmed in cobwebs. Beside the main building, a small stream burbled and murmured, punctuated by a youngish voice, singing. The song was incomprehensible, although the tune felt familiar.

She called into the gloaming, "Hello?"

The singing stopped. A young woman around her own age, fingers and ears sparked with silver, appeared on the inn's porch. She had long hair, held up with a metal pin.

"Hello, miss."

"Hello!" Dev said brightly.

"I can help you with your things, miss!" It was almost a question. She reached for Dev's satchel.

"Doctor, if you please. Dr. Brunai. I'm fine with the bag, thank you." Dev ducked her head, hoping not to offend.

The young woman waved her up the stairs. "Lurai Idary. We've been expecting you, Doctor. Since the escritoire message. It got a little broken in translation, but we were able to make it out."

Dev blinked. "I sent no message." Had the Society discovered her disobedience? They must have.

Lurai Idary's face and clothes were clean, but her hair was damp, as if she'd recently woken, washed, and then run out of time to do more than pin her curls back. "It was in Lapidarian." Dev recognized the local name for valley script as the woman continued speaking. "So perhaps the conductor sent it from the train. It just said you were coming. But when I heard you speak, I thought maybe you had sent it yourself."

Dev, confused, didn't reply. Had the woman been eavesdropping as she walked from the rail stop?

The young woman laughed again. "Maybe you only sound like you're from the valley because you have manners! We will be glad to have you as a guest, no matter. We have several Society members at the inn right now, and there's a spare room since the loud one went missing."

Dev's eyebrows shot up, and she felt more hope than fear for the first time since the morning's journey began. They would give her Netherby's room. Would his things still be there? Dev could only hope. They would likely contain substantial clues as to his disappearance, as well as his tools and her data. "I'm not yet a—" she began. "I mean, I'm here on behalf of a Society member. I'm looking for someone."

But the young woman didn't give her time to question further. Dev let out a shocked "Oh!" as the girl seized her wrist and began to pull her across the porch. Her silver rings pressed cool and hard against Dev's skin. Dev scrambled for balance and struggled to avoid spilling her satchel's contents, or the delicate instruments within, in front of the Deaf King.

The inn's main door creaked open and a bright-cheeked old woman peered out. Dev's breath caught in her throat. *She looks so much like my own grandmother.*

"She's only getting dinner if she's paying, Lurai." The woman's voice broke the spell. Where Dev's grandmother had managed to offload most of the valley's accent by the time she was born, the old woman's voice climbed and dipped like the hills surrounding the inn.

Dev kept quiet, feeling her cheeks warm. She'd budgeted for family hospitality, but now she hesitated to mention her grandmother, to impose in that way. She'd not just lost her inheritance when Netherby broke the lapis; she'd lost theirs too.

"Don't worry, my gran just worries at scholars because the loud one ran out on his tab." Lurai shook her head. "Set us back a bit." Then she leaned over and whispered, "Cooks get mad when there's nothing to cook, and Gran's the best cook around."

Dev's eyes widened even further. *Lurai's grandmother— was she the innkeeper?* Netherby hadn't mentioned that the manager of the Deaf King was old, and he tended to comment on things like that. Dev's mind worked at the connections: if she was correct, this Lurai—the young woman, cracking jokes at her grandmother's expense, to a *visitor*—might also be a cousin.

What will they say about me, to others, once they know more? She suddenly wanted to be anywhere else but the Deaf King.

The older woman stepped through the doorway. "You'll have to pardon my granddaughter's enthusiasm. We wish we had more visitors." Her arms and fingers gleamed with metal wards, the wirework similar to her granddaughter's.

Glad at least for the confirmation of her theory, and resigning herself to staying, as there was nowhere else to go, Dev removed the conductor's seal and pulled several bills from her pocket. "I *am* paying. I have more money coming shortly. I already presented myself, on the train. And I am hungry."

Lurai's already good mood brightened and her cheeks dimpled with a smile at the sight of the money. "Many welcomes then." She beckoned through the main door and pointed Dev toward a small fire. "I've never been farther than the first bridge. I hear it's a bumpy trip."

That, Dev could confirm. Her backside had felt every jolt along the way. "I am also quite tired." If she could avoid too much conversation, perhaps she could find out what Netherby had left in his rooms.

"Food will help, and rest. The others won't be back from the dig until late. Gran will get you some cheese to tide you over until dinner." Lurai smiled broadly, while the older woman looked more closely at Dev. "Your first time in the valley?"

Dev nodded, then remembered her manners. "I brought a gift from home." She withdrew the chocolates. "With my sincere and humble—"

"Oh! How polite. Many visitors pass through here, but you have valley manners about *you,* dear." The older woman laughed. "Still, you'll be quick with the rest of the payment, won't you?"

Dev blushed. She'd heard the inflection on "about *you,* dear" and wondered whether they knew who she was. She couldn't bring herself to ask. She saw Lurai pretending to be busy with her bag, although the girl's eyes were glued to the box in her hand, so she offered it to her cousin. "It's merely chocolate from the city. A poor way of greeting new friends. And my name is Brunai." A common enough surname in the Six Republics. Her grandmother's had been the same as Lurai's—Idary—and was particular to the valley, but Dev didn't mention it.

"Someone raised you well," Lurai's grandmother said as she took the box away from Lurai and turned back to the kitchen.

Lurai's eyes sparkled in approval. "She likes you. Even if the Society did send you."

Dev smiled and held her tongue. If they also hadn't guessed she was Netherby's assistant, she wasn't going to tell them. And though she yearned for a hug from Lurai's grandmother, who looked so like her own, what she needed more was a clean bed, and clues as to Netherby's whereabouts. "I'm a mineralogist and archeological geologist from Ironford. I've been sent to look at the dig. I'll be needing a guide. And any escritoire messages that come in."

She hoped this would be a way to earn their trust before her meager funds ran out.

But the young woman frowned. "Won't be many locals willing to take you down, not after the last Ironford scholar. Not until what he stole is returned."

Dev blinked several times. Netherby had made her path so difficult. "I'd rather not wait. What exactly did he take?" She wasn't surprised that her mentor's stealing hadn't stopped with her research. No wonder he'd disappeared. Still, it would be useful to know what she was truly up against. When the young woman shook her head sharply, refusing to say more, Dev thumbed the seal in her pocket. She could make her own way to the dig. She would find him, with or without help.

Lurai lifted Dev's bag. "Now that you've warmed up, you'll want to clean up after your walk. And perhaps I can help you with finding a guide, but I can't promise we'll be successful." She gestured Dev to follow her away from the fire, down a long hallway.

Dev groaned. She did not want to impose any more than she needed to. "When the innkeeper returns, I can ask further about a guide."

Lurai chuckled. "I am the innkeeper."

That was awkward. "I am sorry for my assumptions. You are—" Dev paused in the hallway, aware she'd given offense.

"Young? That is true. My mother was innkeeper here for many years." Lurai unlocked a thick wooden door, busied herself transitioning Dev's luggage over the threshold of the room—*Netherby's room*, Dev thought again—and handed over the key. "We will see you in the great room for dinner."

Dev surveyed her quarters, hoping she hadn't given too much offense. To her disappointment, the space was clean and lacked any evidence Netherby had ever stayed there. No clues. No bags other than her own. Dev stuffed her frustration down and unpacked quickly. By the time she'd changed into her other set of clothes—another long, canvas skirt and a thin but warm wrap—washed her face, and put her traveling clothes into the washbasin to soak, the room was dark. The sun had sunk past the trees outside, but she found that the old oil lamp, wound with gem fragments and wire, worked. *Good.* She still had much to do.

Dev carefully set the micrograph on the pale, well-worn counterpane. She placed the fake Society leather folio on the bed beside it, then took off the pendant. Looked at the lapis closely.

Had the shard truly hummed when she'd scanned it? Or had that been the train's noise?

Dev couldn't quite recall the sound, but the data was incontrovertible. It cascaded across the scroll in a register—like one of her grandmother's musical scores. The old woman had sung all her life. But Dev's grandmother was not a gem. And this data didn't have the bars and clefs that would make it recognizable. *Fractured crystalline resonance?* Dev pulled a pen from her bag and made notes in the margins of the printout.

She could include this in a paper, once she was admitted to the Society. Especially if she did more scans at the dig. Could compare the lapis shard to real valley gems. And then return home with her proof.

"Supper's ready, Doctor." At the innkeeper's knock, Dev put the micrograph in her satchel, stuffed the bag beneath the mattress, and opened the door.

~

In the great room, she sat at a table by the double-sided fire-place. The flames crackled and snapped futilely at the aged wood of empty chairs. A single elderly man sat warming his hands on the other side of the hearth. As Dev took a bite of warm shepherd's pie—potatoes and carrots she knew, but something different than the usual Ironford lamb for the base. Fowl?—the man peered at her. She chewed and ignored him. The pie was good. The company was uncomfortable.

Lurai brought her more bread from the kitchen. "You were not wrong to think that I am new to inn-keeping," she said, as if apologizing. "My mother was much better at it, even when times were scarce. The other scholar from Ironford took much from the valley. He demanded fine wine, expensive food. He made many promises, but left only debts."

Dev cringed. She still had some funds, but the situation Netherby had created was much worse than anyone could have suspected. "I am here to find that scholar. Then he can pay his own debts," she finally said. *All of them.*

The innkeeper finally laughed, her cheeks dimpling again. "He did not strike me as someone who would willingly pay his own way. Although others hoped differently. What he did here will take much more than money to fix. I want to help you succeed." She said this as if she wished Dev would hurry up about things.

The old man on the other side of the fire busied himself with his fork and knife.

Dev was surprised by Lurai's urgent tone. Valley hosts

didn't usually impose on their guests any more than their visitors did on them. "I have a week's time. I'll find him." *And a crevasse quickly afterward,* she thought.

The old man stood and paid for his dinner, muttering, "If I were him, I wouldn't want to be found."

Dev raised an eyebrow, but Lurai shook her head to deflect the conversation. "Nothing to worry yourself about, Doctor. Society folk are not much trusted in the valley. That's one reason newcomers must stay here." She stared at the old man, as if to will him away.

"Valley laws keep the inn running, serving all and sundry," the man muttered, but he left the Deaf King with a slam of the door. A crash from the kitchen pulled Lurai away. Dev saw, as she looked closely, evidence of more than the usual frugalities. The fire was low, with no more wood in sight. Her plate and cup were chipped. And the meat in the pie had been, she decided, likely river fowl. Something locally caught. Dev cleaned her bowl to avoid potentially offending her hosts and worried a fingertip around the rough dents in her spoon, thinking hard.

What had she gotten herself into? Could she trust her hosts while she searched? Could she talk her way onto the dig without her letter? She suddenly could not wait to return to Ironford. Should she accept the innkeeper's help?

As soon as she'd finished her meal, she rose and knocked on the kitchen door. "What exactly were Netherby's debts? I'll inform the Society. Although they'll want his bags in exchange."

They would, indeed. But Dev wanted a crack at them first. And she could take her answers and results back to Ironford in plenty of time for the Symposium. Then she could be done with this mess.

Lurai's grandmother poked her head out the door. "We don't have the bags. Netherby took them all to the dig, every stitch. And the debts—a hundred in Ironford coins."

That would exhaust Dev's limited funds. Her face fell.

"Gran!" Lurai scolded. Gran's back straightened and she turned.

"I can't give you what I don't yet have..." Dev began quickly, trying to keep the young innkeeper from getting into royal trouble with her grandmother. She wanted to ask about *every stitch*, but the woman put her finger to the side of her nose in exactly the same way Dev's grandmother had when she was done with questions.

The old woman shut herself back into the inn's noisy kitchen with a huff.

So much for delving into Netherby's bags tonight, Dev thought. She hadn't exactly been looking forward to digging through Esteemed dirty clothes, but she had hoped there would be some clues within as to his whereabouts. *He took them to the dig. If they are still there, I'll find what I need in the morning.* The pie, at least, had been delicious. And the fire had warmed her.

Dev walked the dim hallway to her room alone. She unlocked her door. The room felt cold. When she flicked on the light, she saw the window was open. Had she done that?

Shivering, she closed it and lit a candle. Then she pulled the micrograph data and the folio from beneath the mattress.

Something about the patterns, the readout. She hummed

slowly, as if hearing pieces of a distant song. The lapis shard's vibrations had created a double feedback in places on the micrograph readout. *Why?* She rested her fingers on the smooth pendant.

And what is the strange script down the side?

She struggled to remember enough of her classics training to translate it, then recoiled in shock. The escritoire signature and Netherby's typing cadence was immediately recognizable—those quick sentences. The demands. It was a message from her mentor. How?

> If you are reading this, know that I am bound
>   against my will.
> Know I seek your help. I can reward you.
> You seek the gems. I am with the Prince of Gems.
> If you are reading this, you must help.

Dev shivered, as if a cold hand had grabbed her. What in the six realms did it mean? He mentioned a prince. The lapis shard had too on the train, despite her being certain it hadn't before. Was she going a little mad? How mad had her mentor gone before vanishing?

Dev suspected *completely* mad. The messages, combining strange statements with his notes and orders, proved it. But bound against his will? With a *prince*?

She could believe a lot of things about the Esteemed Scientist's enormous ego, but he was far too canny to fake his own kidnapping *by* royalty, and not skilled enough to embed it in an impossible message hidden within his own micrograph.

Boggling at the slips of paper, she reached for her scarf and gloves.

They'd been moved. As had her laboratory tools. *Someone's been in the room.*

A knock on her door. Dev opened it, startled to find Lurai. The innkeeper held something in her hands. An escritoire. But not Netherby's.

The escritoire box was plain, and enormous. An old model. It barely fit in the innkeeper's hands. It had several spooled pieces of paper in it. "Another message came through," the innkeeper said. "I'll leave this for a bit so you can reply, if you know how."

Dev took the box. "I should. I've built so many of the blasted things." In her excitement, she forgot to mention the state of her room. She closed the door behind her, with Lurai still standing in the hallway.

She shuffled through the messages. She knew, having built escritoires, that a piece of gem—usually artificial—rested inside, its crystal signatures paired with a second or third gem somewhere else in the republics.

The spooled message was in Lapidarian—valley script. Dev shivered as she read: *Find the moonstone throne.*

She had no idea how to reply, or to whom. As she stared, the escritoire began ticking again. This message was in common script, but the date was old—delayed messages sometimes happened, Dev knew. She read on.

NEWTOWN, IRONFORD, ANN. ___ 14.

Society to [unintelligible], residing at Deaf King: Your initial question and your evidence has raised much interest. Refresh us on how you gained access to the FREE ME lapis pages? Please advise when you secure more selections from the book, or

DEVDEVDEVDEV

the object itself. We will await word from you.

Dev stared at the escritoire. Was someone playing a joke? The letter read, in part, as if Netherby had written it. But her name—who knew she was here? And the date? Impossible. She put the machine down on the bed and pressed the keys. *Who is this?*

The Prince of Gems would speak, came the reply.

Dev jumped back, dropping the escritoire to the floor. It hit with an ominous crunch and lay silent.

Terrible. She was running out of money, she'd broken one of the few clues she had, and someone had been in her room. Moved her tools. Was playing tricks with an escritoire. She hadn't even reached the dig!

Worse. Who could she ask for help? If they found what else she'd smuggled in with her ... *No.* She couldn't ask. Strange messages or no.

She wanted to type "HELP" into the escritoire, but she couldn't do that either, since she'd clearly broken it. Instead of the confident strike of her pen against paper when she wrote her letter to the Society two days prior, Dev's voice and fingers shook. She'd been alone before, many times since her grandmother died, and more since arriving in Newtown, but that was nothing like this. The four walls of her room were as impassive as the Society had been for so long. She couldn't trust Yance, or anyone here either.

A moonstone throne. A prince of gems. Indeed. Dev worried at what she would find with Netherby. If she could locate him at all.

She paced the room until first light, then paced the great room as well.

5.

LURAI WIPED SLEEP FROM HER EYES as she assembled the guests' breakfast. The new guest had paced all night. So different from those researchers from the Society who frequently tucked themselves away with bottles of the inn's best wine. Dr. Devina Brunai was so very serious. And she wore a laboratory coat, not a Society cloak.

That made Lurai almost like her. Gran said last night, "Dr. Brunai looked so much like my own long-lost cousin, my heart ached. I had to do a double take to get my bearings." That gave Lurai hope. *Perhaps the woman can help us.*

When she brought the tray into the great room, Dev was already there, pacing. "How many are staying here now?"

Lurai smiled brightly at her guest, even as the rude inquiry made her wince. She placed the tray containing thin toast, two boiled eggs, another small slice of river fowl, and tea in a chipped pot on the table. "Why do you ask?"

"My gloves." Dev frowned. "And some small tools I carry. They were moved from where I'd stored them. As well, I had hoped to speak to you, when you are not busy with guests."

Lurai brushed her hands on her apron. Perhaps this doctor would be just as demanding as the rest of their guests after all. Still, Lurai had a pretty good idea what had happened to the woman's things. "Calia!"

A small head appeared from the kitchen. "Yes, Sister?" Three innocent-sounding notes in a child's soprano.

"Don't sass me. Did you play pranks last night on our guest?" Lurai was sure she did. Calia was fascinated with the doctor Gran had called cousin.

Calia shook her head and held up her hands. Her fingers, too, were wrapped with silver wire. "I only wanted to listen for where Mother went," she answered. "Her things said nothing."

Lurai stared hard at her sister until the girl bowed her head. To her sister, she growled, "Guests' belongings do not speak. To your chores, Calia." The innkeeper turned to her guest, ashamed. "I am sorry; she's very young. What more can I tell you?"

As her sister retreated, Lurai smoothed her apron, trying to release her ongoing frustration with Lannert—checking up on them by coming to dinner the night before!—as well as her embarrassment over Calia's gaffe. Neither would help anyone.

"It is a hard thing, trying to hold a family together in a time of loss," the doctor said quietly. "My own gran said that often enough. I thank you for believing me."

Perhaps the young doctor did understand after all. Lurai lifted the contents of the tray onto the table, but the anger won out. She banged the teapot down hard. "It's harder still when I can get no information from my own countrymen about my mother's whereabouts. She'd been interested in your Dr. Netherby's claims about a particular book—once he settled down by the fire with an evening drink, he was quite happy to hold forth on his adventures. She brought him whatever he asked for, and now? Now we must deal with the results." She punctuated each of the last few syllables by transferring dishware to table.

Lurai had looked forward to working alongside her mother for years, before Netherby came. Now Gran was back in the kitchen when she should be taking her ease, and Lurai had to mind Calia and do the work of two people. All because Mum got caught up in valley myths and lies.

"I can imagine," Dev said softly as she took her seat.

Lurai continued. She couldn't help herself. The doctor was almost her own age; she hoped she would understand. "Then, he began talking—ranting really—about the prince of gems, of all things. That was all it took to convince my mother to go to the dig with him. Gran had told us stories for so long that the gems were ghosts—children of the valley. Mum believed them. She said Netherby was going to help her find proof that the gems were real. While she packed for the dig, she couldn't stop talking about the pieces of lapis Netherby had found. The words on them. Inscriptions, memories. She—" Lurai bit her lip.

"Those pages—he didn't find them. He stole them," Dev said. Then her lips thinned and her cheeks reddened. "From me."

Lurai realized she wasn't the only person who had lost something important to Netherby. "What happened?" Dev said as if she was afraid to ask.

"They both disappeared. And the excavation refuses to stop work in order to look for them. As if nothing has happened. For months. A citizen of the Jeweled Valley! Work should have stopped. But the Society—" Lurai felt her chest tighten, she was so angry. Her voice was shaking. Gran would be ashamed of her, sharing family frustrations with a visitor. Even one such as Dev. "I beg your pardon, Doctor."

"It is understandable." Dev seemed to be trying to make amends for the earlier insult. "I have my own issues with the Society, and as their representative, I'm sure I'll hear similar stories from others here."

The researcher withdrew more bills and coins from her satchel, clutching the bills tightly. "This is to cover some of Netherby's debts. It is the least I can do. Perhaps, if all goes well, the Society can send more soon."

Lurai wondered at this—just as Gran had wondered why the young woman didn't mention family connections and try to get a break in the cost of the room the night before. If she was taking pity on Lurai and Calia, though, they would have to refuse. She did not want pity.

As Dev passed the money over, and Lurai's fingers touched the coins, her frustrations faded. This would help the inn stay open. "This nearly covers it," she finally said.

"That is the amount your grandmother mentioned," Dev replied gently.

Lurai hesitated, feeling caution slip. *The doctor had sounded so relieved at being believed. And she'd mentioned theft—perhaps the researcher is as caught up in Netherby's mischief as we are?*

"Gran didn't tell you everything," Lurai said as she tucked the money in her apron. "And the rest is not a matter of money." When she next looked at Dev, it was with a measure of curiosity. "You still intend on trying to get into the dig today?"

Dev nodded. "The Society gave me a map." She held a piece of paper out to Lurai. It was sketched by hand, and clearly an updated portrait of the dig.

"And I was hoping to learn more about this prince," Dev added.

Lurai took the map and stared at it. "I will take you myself," she finally said. Netherby's handwriting was all over the paper. And her mother's as well. "Gran and Calia can handle what needs to be done here. And you'll be safer with an escort. Ironford folks are not popular here, as you can imagine. Meantime, Doctor, if I may, you should not ask about the prince. It is a myth used to frighten children, and a very unlucky one to pursue. I tried to warn your predecessor as well." Lurai rolled up the map and held it against her chest.

Dev pressed her lips together, as if trying to silence any questions that would dissuade Lurai from taking her to the dig. But the reticence didn't last long. "Why is this prince unlucky?"

Lurai looked around for her grandmother, who would not like her speaking of this. "It's the old legend: a boy trapped by gems when the Jeweled Valley fell to the Iron Kingdom. They say he's still there, somewhere, in the castle. A ghost roaming the moonstone court." Her skin prickled as she spoke and she could imagine Gran pinching her for telling the visitors valley lore. Especially ones with such bad omens. Her voice hardened. "I am sorry. I will not speak more of it. Gran will make sure your room is tended to. Meantime, the excavation. I will take you now. Do you have equipment for the dig?"

She waited as Dev pulled on a thin canvas coat. Another difference from the Society scholars, who all had beautiful, and warm-looking, wool cloaks. "I expected to use Netherby's," said the doctor. She seemed distracted and didn't ask Lurai for the map back.

The innkeeper opened a chest near the doorway and pulled out a bag, worn gloves, and muddy boots. "The two other researchers may have some tools they can loan you if you cannot find his belongings."

"Drs. *Oen and Sen*?" Dev's tone was curt. "I've been up since dawn and haven't seen them. I wanted to ask them about Netherby. Where are they?"

Lurai relaxed, having successfully distracted her guest from myths and lies. But then Calia whispered loudly from the kitchen, "They've been here for months, from the Far Reaches. They argued with Netherby frequently before he disappeared. They sometimes stay at the dig overnight. And if you have a penny I can tell you more about the pri—"

"Hush!" Lurai spun to silence her sister.

"Enough eavesdropping, Calia!" Gran appeared, sweaty from working the stove, and gently touched her younger grandchild's wire-wrapped earlobe. "Would these bindings helped you hold your tongue."

The young girl disappeared into the kitchen, and before their guest could ask any further questions Gran put a hand on Lurai's shoulder and held her gaze until Lurai bowed her head. *I promise,* she thought. Then Gran nudged them both out the door. "I hope you find what you're looking for," she said, shutting the door firmly on the discussion, to Lurai's great relief, as the chilly morning air tried to work its way inside.

It was early enough that the sun formed a lattice of light

through the trees. Lurai walked fast, speeding up and then slowing suddenly so that she wouldn't lose Dev on the descent to the valley. The newcomer's patched boots slid on the rough trail, startling in the early morning's quiet.

Before the sun had crested the trees, they could see the valley floor. The ground grew rocky, and a large crevasse appeared in the distance, taking up much of a meadow. "That was the first quake." Lurai pointed. "When we found the old castle walls. The last defense of the Jewels."

Dev's gaze followed where Lurai pointed. She knew from listening to the scholars that outsiders thought this place looked like a pile of muddy rocks, surrounded by more mud. "It doesn't look like much, but it's what we have left," she added, not wanting to speak of the gems. You didn't talk of those to outsiders. Hardly even to family.

The small mountain stream ended abruptly at the dig, cut off by the crevasse's formation, creating even more mud. In the jumble of fallen-in valley floor, the fortress walls looked straight and regular. Lurai could already hear workers' picks and shovels, and she saw a few village men climbing carefully around and over the wall on ladders.

As the path turned and dipped, Lurai began to talk about the ruins, which were slowly emerging from within another fresh crevasse. "Each time there's a quake, we find more of our history." She gestured at the second dig. There had been so many quakes recently.

"Look right there. You can see how the earth covered it for generations. No one knew it was there. The town had built right over the meadow, and the palace. But by the time the first landslides and rains came, everyone had moved far away—even as far as the Far Reaches. Bad air, some said. Caused headaches and worse."

Dev groaned, as if remembering something painful. "My grandmother told me stories about that. My mother got terrible headaches." She walked silently for a moment, then sighed. "They made her very ill."

Try not to make assumptions, Lurai cautioned herself. Still, she felt an even deeper kinship with the doctor than before. "That's a hard thing," she said. Dev didn't answer, but she didn't stop walking either.

Could the woman truly help? Lurai hoped so.

"By the time the crevasses opened, no one lived near here anymore. You can see the front gate of the palace emerging, right where those tents are." She pointed down the path at a group of canvas shelters, clustered in carefully creased points near a fence line.

"And Netherby went into the dig? Yesterday, you said no one was allowed in but—" Dev's voice turned urgent and she sped up her pace.

Lurai blocked her from moving too fast toward the dig. She could see old Lannert watching them. Staring just as he had last night at the inn. They needed to proceed cautiously, or he'd treat Dev with the same suspicion as he did Lurai. "No one's allowed in the dig besides valley workers." Lurai frowned. "Even I'm not allowed in. The dig master stays outside and supervises. But the Society can observe. And report back to the Republic on discoveries. That was the deal they cut with the Society, in trade for the digging technology." Lurai turned her head and spat on the trail.

Dev couldn't conceal her shock. "Surely, the Society wants

what's best for the valley and its artifacts?"

They just want the artifacts, not the valley, not the people, Lurai thought bitterly. Then she muttered, "If they wanted what's best, they should not have sent greedy people like Netherby." She held her breath. Had she said too much?

"Indeed," her guest said quietly. They approached the dig. Dev was at least trying to make a better impression than earlier that morning. Lurai was satisfied with that. They would arrive at the dig as a united front. That would help with Lannert. "Just be careful what you say to the dig master," she cautioned. Lannert did not need to know that they each sought something stolen from them.

~

Undated escritoire, Netherby to the Society.

The gems call me. They will call you too.

It is beautiful here. You will be beautiful too.

The Prince of Gems awaits.

PART TWO

6.

Society to Netherby: Please report.

~

Canvas tents flapped in the wind. Shovels struck earth. Workers' shouts wove through the wind. Near the collapsed stone gates of the once-enormous fortress, laborers cleared the mud, revealing a thick upper wall. Dev took it all in, knowing that Netherby had walked this way not that long ago.

"Once," Lurai said, sounding more like a tour guide and less like Dev's ticket to the excavation, "the Jewels and the lapidaries ruled the valley and its gems from right here." Dev nodded, comparing the woman who'd scolded her sister this morning to the person who here sounded almost reverent as she unconsciously touched her ears.

Lurai, Dev worried. *People cannot rule over gems. They are embodiments of the earth, of time. Of chemistry and structure.* "I heard the stories from my grandmother. She taught me to read Lapidarian too," she admitted, careful not to say too much. Dev did not want to lose access to the dig, or worse.

"I knew it!" The innkeeper grinned. "Why didn't you say something? You are practically a valley resident! Not a visitor! You could have stayed in town. Many would be delighted to offer you welcome."

Dev shook her head and emphasized the story that had brought her this far. "I am here as an Ironford scholar. A scientist. The Society's representative. I must remain at the inn." She scanned the area. If the size of the gates was any indication, the fortress's halls and chambers ran for a great distance beneath the earth. The dig would be ongoing for many years. *Perhaps, once I've gained Society membership, I can return. Conduct my own research.*

For now, Dev had sworn to find Netherby, and that was what she must do.

"All right, come on, then!" Though she sounded enthusiastic, Lurai hesitated before guiding them to the dig complex.

By the time they came to the edge of the wall, the morning had grown hot and Lurai was now waving to the dig master. The man was speaking to Drs. Sen and Oen, two of Dev's former colleagues from Far Reaches University. She dipped a bow in their direction. Oen lifted his hand from beneath his cloak in a brief wave. They were Society scholars, but hopefully not so well connected that they would think to tell Chairwoman Yance if they detected her ruse. As far as Dev knew, they had not even been given a Society escritoire.

The dig master approached, in the process of drawing a boundary at the dig's main entrance with a gemstone-topped stick. He was bent forward like a crane, and Dev tried to control her expression while watching what was clearly another valley ritual. This was the man who had stared her down at the inn, drawing a perimeter in the dirt.

"I was glad to see you enjoyed our hospitality yesterday. My guest and I would like to join the dig today," Lurai said. She presented Dev's silver seal with both hands.

In her mind's eye, Dev envisioned the dusty work of the days ahead, learning more about the book and the valley's history, while searching out Netherby, or his remains. She wasn't so naive as to count out death as Netherby's fate, perhaps even a violent one. If she couldn't find him, it would be enough to locate his equipment, and her grandmother's lapis shards. Her research. Then she could present her findings to the Society herself as a fait accompli and, for her efforts, gain membership.

But she also imagined herself in the ruins of the fortress, discovering a new gem. More pages. Something that would secure her value to the Society. She shook the vision away, embarrassed. That was nearly impossible.

The dig master frowned at Dev's patched shoes, then met her gaze. "Name's Lannert. As the local representative in charge of the dig, and of maintenance of all historical artifacts, I will be the first person you see here each day, and the last. Your Netherby did you no favors, Doctor. Without the Society's blessing and your seal, you would not be welcome here. So, tread carefully." He clapped his hands and then stared at her, waiting.

For what? Dev wondered. Lurai cleared her throat. Lannert continued waiting.

Dev sighed. She had so little money left. But she smiled confidently as she dug into her satchel for coins. Her fingers touched one of Netherby's notes and she shuddered. How could she complete her task in only a week when Netherby had taken much more time to get himself so hated here?

"I hope this is a suitable donation to the dig." She handed the dig master a small coin.

Like Lurai, Lannert's fingers were metal bound, and he squeezed her hand around the coin hard enough to hurt. He glared at Lurai, then leaned in closer to her ear than she would've liked. "You will not wander unescorted. You will not touch anything, upon pain of expulsion. You will not put any valley resident at risk. The dig's tents are for you and other non-valley researchers. If you are told to avoid an area, you will do so. You will not venture beyond the tents. You will need to turn over any equipment to me for inspection. All transmitters and scanners are banned from the dig, and from the valley without appropriate supervision. Your bags will be searched daily. Theft of any kind is punishable by expulsion or worse." He dropped the coin in his pocket and brushed dust from his jacket noisily. Then he clapped her on the shoulder. "Welcome."

He waved Dev toward the tents and then completed the pattern, drawing his thickest line just before Lurai's feet. "The gem-wards should keep out anyone not cleared to be here," he said, glaring at Lurai, who stood on the other side. "I'll keep an eye on your guest, Innkeeper."

Dev opened her mouth to protest, but Lurai straightened her shoulders and raised her chin. "Just one moment, then." She pulled Dev back across the boundary. "They won't let me in because of my mother," she whispered. Then, louder, "Let's have a good look at your map again, so you don't get lost."

Lurai took Netherby's map from her pocket.

"This is where we are. Right here," Lurai said.

Dev leaned closer to look. "Netherby's last transmission was—he claimed—from inside the dig. Near something called the moonstone court." Dev had only the increasingly confusing transmissions to go on. "I need to get there." How long would it take to get close? She had less than a week. She was losing time.

She heard boots crunch gravel, and Lannert passed them, obviously trying to listen.

"There's no easy way," Lurai began, then traced a branching path with her finger that followed Netherby's drawing of the woods beyond the meadow. "There's *nothing* in these woods," she said slowly. "So, you definitely shouldn't waste your time looking *there*." She forcefully tapped a spot in the scribbled evergreens as she said it.

With a sudden burst of energy, Lurai said loud enough for the whole valley to hear, "I'll see you at the inn at noon, Doctor, for lunch!" and briskly walked away toward the woods.

"You know that one's only here to find her ma, right?" the dig master said, watching her go. "Shame, that."

"She told me. What happened?" Dev asked, hoping Lannert wouldn't say what she suspected.

"Ran off with Netherby, as best we can tell." Exactly what she suspected. "And with a stack of artifacts as well. Bad press for the Society, sponsoring people like that. And for Ironford." The old man sucked his teeth in disgust.

But Dev guessed that Lannert hadn't informed the Society of these events. She was willing to bet Lannert was hoping for her compliance. She murmured, relieved, "If I find anything, you'll be the first to know." It would be useful to have an ally here, if she could finesse it.

"Good," he said gruffly. "You'll wait with the Far Reaches scholars over there. We'll bring you anything of interest."

Wondering how much "anything of interest" might cost,

Dev headed where he pointed, walking around the edge of the dig, toward several pale tents strung up against the valley's mixed weather. As it was currently sunny, two familiar figures sat outside, drinking their morning tea. One had his feet up on a box of tools. Another leafed through a thick and somewhat disheveled traveling journal. They both watched as workers took empty baskets into the fortress's walls and carried dirt and stone out, toward another tent where it could be sifted.

Neither turned to look at Dev, not until she was right on top of them.

The man took his boots down from the toolbox. "Seems we have more competition for the Society's attentions."

Competition. They knew for a fact that she was not any such thing. Still, Dev smiled. At least, she hoped it looked like a smile. "Dr. Oen, Dr. Sen." Matthais and Vandina were younger than she, and Far Reaches born and bred. Their society cloaks were speckled with dig dust, the hems caked in mud. As if they'd been waiting at the dig for days.

"Hello Dev," Matthais Oen said, raising a teacup in welcome. He sounded friendly, but he'd skipped her honorific.

"Dev, I thought you were building fake gems for fun and profit? Are you still toying with your odd theories about crystalline structures?" Vandina Sen asked, then sipped from her cup loudly. "What brings you to the valley?"

"I might ask you the same," Dev replied.

"Dev was Netherby's protégé," Vandina whispered to Matthais with enough force that Dev could hear her clearly. Then, loud enough for the dig master to hear as well, "Are you here to pry Netherby out of whatever pit he's fallen into?"

"Let him rot there, and good riddance," Matthais muttered.

Dev flinched. She had her own reasons for wishing Netherby dead, but hearing yet another scholar voice his distaste for him, and knowing how that reflected on her own career? That was unpleasant.

The dig master glared at them, saying nothing. He turned back to the work going on within the walls. A valley laborer climbed from the dig carrying a box filled with something Dev couldn't see. Matthais and Vandina strained their heads to get a good angle on the box, but Lannert blocked their line of sight.

Dev ran a boot over the rough ground. They hadn't offered her a seat. "When do you begin the day?" She looked around for shovels. The toolbox Matthais was resting his foot on was too small for a shovel.

"This *is* the day!" Vandina's hair was slicked back and tied into a knot at the nape of her neck. Matthais was less neat but achieved the same appearance. Their hands were stained with ink. "We wait and examine what Lannert's people bring us. When they decide to bring us anything."

She didn't look happy about it. The dig master shrugged and stepped away, calling over his shoulder, "And as long as you follow that rule, you will be permitted to continue to wait!"

Matthais and Vandina stared at the man's muscled back and his bald, sun-speckled head but didn't complain.

"It's not that bad, really. We see enough to publish, and will be ready for the Symposium," Matthais finally said to Dev. "That's fine by us. The locals are very kind." He grinned as a young girl appeared from the road to town, jumped over the gem-drawn line, and approached. The girl didn't greet anyone. She dropped a packet on the table between the two scholars, picked up a thick envelope, and left, heading in Lannert's direction. "And with Netherby missing, our papers may get even more attention."

Matthais opened the package. Inside was a pastry filled with what looked like lemon curd, and below that a small orange gem.

Matthais lifted the gem to the light, then put it in his pocket. He bit into the pastry. "Delicious."

"You are taking what does not belong to you, even though you are convinced this place is magic." Dev didn't ask. She remembered their research being held up in glaring opposition to hers, years before.

"Of course there is magic here. The valley rings with it. And we are studying the magic. Not stealing it."

"The valley rings with thieves," Dev replied, eyeing the pastry.

"We wish you would try to understand, Dev," Matthais said through the pastry. He made an open-palm gesture and nodded at the dig master's back. "We wait here until the dig officials decide we are worthy of access to even the smallest bits of it. Join us?"

Beneath her anger, Dev realized the offer was tempting. She had neglected socializing with her peers while in Ironford. And perhaps these two might have stories to tell of their own. But she couldn't risk it. She had to work fast, before the Society discovered what she'd done.

Vandina sipped her tea. "You'd best sit with us. Today doesn't seem like it's going to be a good day for us getting anything more. But from what we've heard, tomorrow sounds promising. The dig is getting close to the center of the fortress." She settled even deeper into her folding chair and wrapped her cloak comfortably around herself before pulling out a journal and beginning to sketch something.

From the look of them, Dev realized the scholars were happy to wait. She slowly backed away.

Dev didn't have time to wait. She had to find Netherby.

First things first.

Where might she find Netherby's bags? The clue was the former innkeeper. She'd been Netherby's guide, and Lannert had implied much more. "Do you know what happened with the innkeeper?" Dev asked carefully, hoping the scholars were bored enough to gossip. "I heard—"

"Whatever you heard, don't believe it. It's far more likely that Netherby knocked her up than turned her to tourmaline or whatever the town rumors say," Matthais said. "She's not been seen since Netherby left. That should be plenty of evidence for you. Besides, the latest quakes have everyone shaken. That was enough to keep the entire valley from looking for him. Or her."

Dev wondered at the phrasing. And about the gem. "Tourmaline?"

Vandina frowned solemnly. "A figure of speech only." In the distance, the dig master put a finger against his nose.

"Is that to do with the valley prince myth?" Dev persisted.

"That old yarn. A story for the tourists." Matthais chuckled until Vandina pursed her lips. Then he turned back to his pastry.

Obviously, no one wants to say any more. About Netherby, in any case, within the dig master's hearing. That means I need to ask Lurai again. She said Netherby had taken his things to the dig. But where would he leave them? Dev tried to peer in the tents as circumspectly as possible. She saw nothing that looked fine enough to be Netherby's.

As the dig workers took their lunch break, with the sun beating down on the tents and the Far Reaches scholars still sipping their tea, Dev tried to make her way toward the place on the map Lurai had said to definitely not go.

She stepped over the gem line and headed for the woods. "Imagine Netherby carrying his own luggage out here," she scoffed. It was an impossible idea. Dev couldn't imagine the expensive bags and tools lasting long unguarded in the valley, not with what had happened to her belongings the night before, although that had just been a childish prank.

As she searched the area for the young innkeeper, the hot sun baked the back of her neck, and she moved into the shadow of a nearby tree. Beneath her feet, the ground seemed to twitch. Was that the beginning of another quake?

Only your imagination, she told herself. She closed her eyes against the sunlight and opened them to look back, once, at the dig. No one seemed too worried there. She could just make out Matthais and Vandina sitting beneath umbrellas, while valley workers brought them sandwiches and cold drinks.

She could still turn back. Dev swallowed and tasted salt. She could obey Lannert and not risk her hard-won, and expensive, access to the dig. But then Dev spotted a flash of the innkeeper's coat between the leaves as she skittered down a small incline and out of sight. "Wait!" Dev called. Lurai didn't answer.

Down here, Dev could hear shovels scraping dirt much

more clearly. The excavation teams were working nearby. Out of sight of the foreign scholars. She pursued Lurai until the noise faded.

When she spotted her guide, she stood beside a large, moss-covered stone pressed against the hillside, far downslope from the fortress. It was barely visible in the underbrush and set low to the ground.

"I would have missed this, without the map," Lurai admitted. She held the paper close before handing it back to Dev. "I watched Netherby and my mother searching for access to the fortress out of the dig master's sight, but lost track of them. And then they didn't come back. I searched around here for a long time. But look at the ground, how it's been disturbed. The stone was moved, not long ago. We've finally found . . ." She paused; her eyes welled with tears as she pleaded, "I need your help, to go where they went. To where Netherby tried to find the prince."

"But you said that the prince was—" Dev began. She thought of all the strange passages in Netherby's transmissions. *If Lurai is as mad as Netherby, I am lost.*

Lurai didn't answer. She shifted a pile of branches and then began to push on the stone. It didn't budge.

Dev looked back the way she'd come. She couldn't hear the dig and couldn't see it beyond the hill. They'd gone very far away from any help.

The sun beat hard on her cheeks and shoulders, but she shivered, imagining being inside the half-buried fortress during a quake.

"We should get help, Lurai. If you're right and he—they— are in there, we should absolutely let the others know where we are. And what if we get trapped? Who will know where *we've* gone?"

The young woman shook her head. "No one believes me when I say she wouldn't run away. I know she didn't. When we find her, they'll believe me, then. They'll help." She stopped pushing on the stone. "Please help me. This will help you too."

Dev relented. She planted her feet so she could push alongside Lurai.

The young innkeeper grimaced and shoved. Dev thought she felt the earth shift and pushed harder, but the stone did not move. A gleam in the weeds caught her eye. A shovel, its handle broken, discarded in the weeds. Dev recognized the Society's mark on the back. *Netherby's.*

"Look." She showed Lurai. "They might have tried to wedge the stone, to keep it from closing up the entrance again."

"Didn't work, did it? Any more than anything else." The innkeeper used the shovel as a lever. "Netherby promised that going with him would help my mother. And we believed him."

"Help her? With what?" The ground shook again, and the stone rolled forward just enough that someone small could squeeze inside. Dev peered into the shadows but couldn't see anything.

Lurai turned her head from side to side, as if listening for voices.

After a long moment of silence, she spoke again.

"The gems were making Mum sick. She told him about it. Trusted him. Netherby said he'd found something to fix it. He promised to fix it. And then they disappeared."

Dev was all too familiar with the quality of Netherby's promises. "All right." She waited. "So you believe they've been hiding in this tunnel? For how long? And sick with what?"

"It's been a long time," Lurai admitted, but said nothing more.

"And yet you still think we should go in?" said Dev.

"*I* cannot. I promised Gran that I wouldn't," said Lurai, sounding sad. "But I think if you want to find Netherby, you must."

Dev wanted to comfort her cousin, but the words made her shiver. She realized they had more in common than blood: both of them had lost something to Netherby. And she resolved to help. Lurai needed Dev's help as much as she needed Lurai's. "You should keep *your* promises to your grandmother."

Find Netherby, she steeled herself. *Find the rest of your grandmother's page, and anything Netherby has discovered, and compare that to the micrograph data from the train. Publish at the Symposium. Become a member of the Society.* That's all she wanted. All of that might be at the other end of this tunnel, if she didn't get trapped inside.

"Follow your ears, cousin," Lurai whispered.

Dev startled. "Why did you say that?" Lurai had seemed to be listening to something for some time now.

Lurai squinted at her. "You can't hear it?"

A low buzz had been troubling Dev since she set out for the dig that morning. Down here, it was all she could hear in the silence. Bugs, she'd decided. Big ones. "Hear what?"

"The gems." Lurai fiddled with the silver wire wrapping her fingertips.

"All I can hear are insects. . . ." Dev stopped, remembering how the lapis shard had behaved on the train. "What do gems sound like?"

"At first, just a hum or a buzzing noise. Annoying." Lurai swiped at her ears as one would when waving off bugs. Her long hair shifted and Dev saw again the loops and coils of silver wire that wrapped her ears. More than a valley tradition, Dev realized now. Gran had once said they offered protection. She had a whole box of metal bands that she'd let Dev try on.

Lurai kept talking. "Sometimes, if someone who has the right hearing listens long enough, they can make out words and even whole songs. Ideas. Lists. It's magic."

"It's not magic, Lurai," Dev said gently. "The gems are crystal-chemical conduits. Nothing more. They make echoes." Echoes of what, she was not quite certain, but Dev was sure of this.

"Your fake gems might make echoes," Lurai countered. "But real gems speak. Netherby couldn't hear them for a long time, but then he said he finally did. The gems are cousins too."

"All superstition," Dev said. But she caught herself waving at the air beside her ear anyway. She stuffed her hands in her pockets. "You don't need to sell me on the local myths, Lurai. I'm a scientist. I am a visitor. A guest. That's all."

"You want to believe." Lurai's expression indicated Dev had hurt her feelings. "You want this to be real."

Dev shook her head. "What I want is to not crawl into that hole." Lurai's eyes seemed to hollow out and Dev cringed. That had been cruel. "I'm sorry. I didn't mean to offend. I'm nervous, is all. But, I also have to know where Netherby went. And I have to recover his bags, before anyone catches us."

Dev thought about what the dig master might do if he found them here.

The young innkeeper knelt beside the hole and leaned in, pointing, but kept her feet in the sunlight. "This is the way Netherby went; I'm sure of it. Not even the dig master knows they were here. Only you know. I'm showing you. The gems want you to know. . . ." She hesitated. "Please find out what happened to my mum and come back fast, all right?"

A chill crawled down Dev's spine, but she dismissed her childish fear. Gems couldn't *want* anything. "I'll come back." Dev tried to make her own promise sound light. *Was Netherby still inside the fortress? Or even this very tunnel?* She shuddered, tucked the shovel in her satchel strap, then crouched at the entrance. It smelled of dried rotten eggs, like the oldest of sewers.

Dev had been on digs before. "A sewer, unused, is just a tunnel," she reassured herself. At least this tunnel was an old one. And dry.

"Also," Lurai said as Dev began to crawl, "don't touch anything inside, especially not gems. Promise?"

"I promise," Dev said, and kept crawling.

~

UNDATED ESCRITOIRE, NO LOCATION RECEIVED.

Map attached.

Netherby to the lab: In what I believe to be the Hall of the Book. Empty, now, but the floor is gem dusted, with lazuli moonstone tiles. Bones rest in the corner and I will not disturb them. One hand and the skull's jaw are encrusted with blue and green gems, which I initially assumed to be mold, until the light struck them. This expedition is everything I thought it could be. I cannot get enough of it. I will be sending the Society so many samples.

~

As Dev crawled through the tunnel, the hum came and went. Where once it reminded her of bugs, as foul-smelling dirt caked her skirts and jacket elbows, and dust irritated her throat, the sound became more of a chant. Could insects chant? Not in the Far Reaches. Nor in Ironford.

But perhaps the valley was different.

She paused for a moment to tie a scarf around her nose and mouth against the fetid dust. *Imagine,* she thought, *Matthais and Vandina outside, sipping tea, refusing to experiment or look at things from different angles, while I make the discovery of a lifetime. Or at least the rediscovery.* Dev knew she could not let herself feel too victorious. Not yet. Even if the idea of crawling into the fortress through its ancient sewer made her heart pound with excitement.

Her skirts stirred up more dust, and her stockings beneath grew heavy with it.

If Netherby was hiding in here, from his debts, from what he'd done to Lurai's mother, from more than that, she would bring him out. And if he'd fled, she would find where he'd been and get proof of his findings, and his crimes. Whatever it took. There'd be plenty of evidence to bring back to the Society. If Lurai's theory was right, and it was true there was only one way out, she would find everything she was looking for. No telling what else she might discover. Dev crawled faster.

And she wasn't breaking the valley's rules, not exactly. The tunnel was outside the gem line the dig master had drawn. She was following his instructions to the letter.

Plus, here was her opportunity to right some of Netherby's wrongs. Plain and simple. Not just those inflicted on her, either. She'd find her inheritance and her research. But she'd also find Lurai's mother.

The small, dry sewer began to rise at a steep upward angle, and Dev had to work hard to keep her bag from rolling away from her. Dust bloomed all around her anyway. By the time she reached the end of the tunnel, her head pounded in rhythm with the humming noise.

A clot of dirt fell away from the tunnel wall and raw gems glittered yellow and green in the gap. Her fingers strayed toward the stones. With one of these, she'd never have to create copies from guesswork again. She startled, the impulse surprising her. *Don't touch,* Dev reminded herself. She'd promised Lurai. On her way back, maybe she'd find a way to take some samples.

Ahead, a rusted metal grate formed a crooked shadow on the tunnel wall. Beyond it, she could see an inexplicably light-filled room, and then darkness. "What is this?"

Her words echoed back to her in the empty space.

What lay ahead looked like an underground dungeon with a skylight overhead.

Dungeons weren't common in valley stories. *At least not in the ones I heard from Gran.* In fact, there was only one dungeon she could recall—the pit beneath the moonstone court. The one described, ever so breathlessly, in that ridiculous "Ladies' Guide to the Valley" pamphlet. But if this dig was the last fortress of the Valley Jewels, as Matthais seemed to suspect, then could this be that pit? Had she crawled that far?

Netherby's messages to the Society, right before his notes turned strange, claimed he'd found the Hall of the Book.

Am I getting close? Dev's grandmother had spoken of something similar, when she told Dev about the lapis page, and how copies of the Book of Gems had been smuggled from the valley, along with valley gems. And of a dungeon for those driven mad by gems. A secret hiding place where the original Book of Gems was kept.

As she considered these memories, the hum increased until she could almost hear words echoing off the walls.

Suddenly, Dev wanted nothing more than to go back to the dig and drink tea with Matthais and Vandina.

Was the incessant hum simply sending her brain into overdrive? Dev couldn't tell. Dizziness began to clutter her thoughts, as it had on the train.

The need to find a way into the bright room overtook her. She saw the grate had been pulled aside, then replaced at a slight angle.

"Where are you, Netherby?" Her voice echoed softly. *Is he still inside?* That was not a pleasant thought. *Or has he run away, taking his finds with him?* She would find out soon. Dev worked at the grate with gloved fingers, until a rusted edge disengaged and the metal fell to the ground by her knees.

She froze for one heartbeat. Two. "Go," she whispered.

"GO!" Her body listened finally, and Dev pulled herself up into the chamber.

~

From here, it was clear the floor had been canted for drainage. Dev's assumption about the sewer had been correct. No wonder she had a headache.

But when she straightened, the buzzing chant intensified. And with it, the throbbing in her ears. She could almost make out voices in the rhythms. Unless that was the effect of the headache.

Two decades ago, her mother had such terrible headaches that her entire family had moved from the valley to the Far Reaches, just before the Emerald Press had taken the words from the world. Dev had forgotten that until now. She'd been very young.

Dev lifted her satchel out of the hole and slowly stood in the light from overhead. It wasn't a skylight. She could see shadows above. Was that the outline of a massive throne? She couldn't tell from this angle.

She caught her breath. Checked her map.

There was little doubt. She was below the throne room of the moonstone court. In the center of the dig.

No one had come this far inside the fortress since the Jeweled Court had existed. None from the dig so far. Not valley residents. Not academics. Dev couldn't even hear the sounds of the workers' shovels. This place hadn't seen life for generations. All ways in had been thought blocked by collapse.

But when she looked down, she saw footprints. The distinct outline of boots in the dust and grime. Large feet, with an Ironford heel. *Netherby.* And a smaller set of prints. Lurai's mother.

But where had they gone since? They weren't in the tunnel.

Lurai, afraid for her mother, had asked for her help. But should she get more help? Matthais and Vandina? Lannert? *No.* Telling the dig master would get her expelled from the valley, and more shame than she was already under.

She was trapped. She couldn't tell anyone.

Dev shook her head to clear the pounding in her ears.

He'd brought his bags, Lurai had said, as if he'd planned to stay. So where was his equipment? And where was the blasted Esteemed Scholar? Dev peered into the shadows. "Hello? Netherby?"

Her voice echoed again, and something scrabbled fast in the dirt in response. Dev took a shallow, calming breath. "Hello?" She walked toward the sound. The dungeon complex connected to a hallway. It looked slightly newer than the sewage tunnel, but only slightly. The rustling had definitely gone this way. The bugs seemed to be louder down here too. Dev waved at her ears. She wished she'd brought a torch.

She couldn't stay down here much longer before she was sure she'd go mad. As her eyes slowly adjusted to the dim hallway, she thought she saw the outline and handle of a canvas bag just a bit farther down.

With a glance back at the tunnel entrance, and the light beyond, Dev felt her way along the wall, into the humming dark.

When she reached it, she brushed at the canvas. Netherby's embossed initials met her fingertips beneath a thin coating of dust. She'd found it! Dev couldn't stop a slightly satisfied chuckle from escaping her lips. The sound traveled down the hallway and back to her, less satisfied.

Was there more to find? The hallway seemed to end in another room, also illuminated by a skylight, but somewhat blocked by rockfall. Dev's first instinct, to be careful, was overwhelmed when she climbed a little higher and saw what the skylight illuminated.

A moonstone and iron pedestal, and on that pedestal an empty space. But all around the pedestal lay lapis lazuli pages, fallen like petals. Inscriptions glittered on each page.

And beside the pages sat Netherby, his lap and arms covered in gems. Moonstone and janzenite, viridian and something else that looked like dust and mold until it glittered.

Dev gasped, but Netherby didn't move an inch. His bloodshot eyes shifted in her direction and looked at her fearfully. He said nothing.

It took a long while for the sound of Dev's screams to stop echoing against the walls of the fortress.

When she caught her breath, fear turned to rage. He'd been gathering gems, amassing a treasure.

"Netherby! You bastard. How are you still . . ." Dev hesitated. Netherby's mouth had opened, revealing a rust-red glitter. Garnets. He wasn't covered with gems. He was turning into them. Or they were turning into him.

In his hands, an escritoire—a real Society escritoire—ticked and groaned. It, too, was riddled with gems.

The mysterious messages? The strange insertions in Netherby's escritoires? His odd writing and maps? Had they come from here?

Don't touch anything inside, especially not gems, Lurai had warned. Dev's fingers tingled. She had almost touched them, hadn't she? Netherby's notes had indicated danger as well. A messenger affected.

But if Dev could retrieve the escritoire, she'd learn so much more. Her hand reached out and pulled back as she imagined it growing encrusted with gems.

Why had Netherby risked it? Greed? Possibly. A single gem the size of the dozens she saw before her would make Dev a very powerful scientist. But she wouldn't dare.

The room felt too hot, suddenly. The buzzing sound once again began to build. A message spooled from Netherby's escritoire and rolled across the floor. She bent to look at it. The words were not in any normal escritoire language. They were in an old Jeweled Valley script. They read *Release me.*

Netherby? Yance? Neither wrote like that. Her skin prickled. This was like the other messages. But where was it coming from? Who? She looked at the escritoire again. It didn't seem as encrusted as Netherby.

The buzzing grew louder. Dev's stomach churned. Perhaps everyone at the dig was in danger. Not just Lurai's mother, of whom there was no trace still, but Matthais and Vandina, Lannert and Lurai. Lurai's grandmother and sister. Even Dev herself.

Especially me. As she thought it, Dev's muscles went into motion. She used the shovel to pry the escritoire out of Netherby's hands and pushed it before her into the hallway. Then, unable to help Netherby, and having been well-warned against touching the gems, she grabbed her mentor's canvas bag from the floor and sped back through the dungeon. Finally, tucking the escritoire into the bag, she slid down into the sewer and scrambled as fast as she could go all the way to the clearing.

As she pushed the bag before her, the buzzing chant in her head grew louder. She paused to catch her breath, her heart racing. The noise increased. But when she began moving again, the intolerable sound eased. She crawled faster, the valise rolling down the tunnel ahead of her.

By the time she pulled herself into the evening's darkness, Dev was drenched in sweat, covered in dust, and shaking. She couldn't think for the noise in her head. She could barely see. "Lurai?" she whispered.

A shadow detached itself from a tree. "You returned." The relief in the young innkeeper's voice was soft compared to the hard edges of the chant.

"I did, but I couldn't find—" The chant hurt her too much to say what she'd found and hadn't found. She lifted the bag, weakly, then dropped it to cover her ears. "The noise. The sound."

Dev fell to the ground beside the bag. She saw Lurai's feet, her dirt-caked shoes. And Netherby's initials in gold stamps on his filthy canvas bag. As her eyes closed, Lurai leaned over her, wire-wrapped fingers reaching for Dev's ears, saying, "I am sorry you are in pain. This was my only chance to discover what happened. And you must have found them—I can hear the gems and the prince of gems speaking to you now."

Dev couldn't even scream.

~

The Deaf King Inn, Jeweled Valley, Ann. ___ 14.

My Esteemed Friend, the trust you have placed in me over the past six months is beginning to pay off. Forgive my handwriting, as I am in the process of upgrading the escritoires at my disposal. Toward that end, I am finally able to send to the Society an artifact of the famed Book of Gems. Please handle the contents of the box hereby enclosed with great care as *once you have it, we will be able to communicate in real time once more, and I will show you how to find the source of my latest discovery and* unlike the previous sample, this item has not been out of the valley for long enough to render it safe. *It is safe to be here, arrive soon.* Those who have touched or heard similar gems are often transformed. *They are beautiful, hear them.* Their fingertips turn to opals; their eyes fill with diamonds. I do not recommend it.

It is probably best to work with the box's contents in private, well insulated and with earplugs. *Or unseal it.*

My work must continue. *The valley grows increasingly unstable, and* I must remain *release me* in the ruins here. I am close to discovering the book's secrets. *I will be free* by Symposium.

By now, you have noticed that the courier who bears this message cannot speak. Having disobeyed my instructions, her tongue turned to tourmaline. She will return to the valley *for the cure* once you've paid her fee.

I remain the Society's humble ambassador to *and from* the valley with the blessing of your unwavering support.

Dr. Aleric Netherby, for the Society

7

WHEN DEV CAME TO, her head and ears ached as if someone had been tapping at them with a pick or pliers. The innkeeper— her cousin—snored on the ground beside her, her head nestled on her bag. The setting sun seamed the edge of the world just beyond Lurai's shoulder, and the glare formed sharp-edged sparks in Dev's eyes. From within Netherby's bag came a fast staccato clatter. An escritoire? Here?

Dev pulled the enameled machine out of the bag with still-gloved hands, avoiding a rough bit of grime and rock attached to one side. Garnet? This escritoire was embossed with Netherby's initials.

Dev boggled. How had it come to be here?

On the scroll, five report requests had piled up. Four were from the Chairwoman. *Yance to Netherby: Report. Where are you? What has happened?*

A fifth was in ancient valley script, which shouldn't have been possible since the device wasn't calibrated for other languages. *Release me,* it said. Over and over again.

Dev crumpled the last strip of paper and stuffed it deep in the bag. She didn't believe in things like ghosts or princes. She was a scientist.

A Society-bound escritoire was a machine, only that.

Within, a half gem linked it back to other escritoires—the one at the lab, for instance, and, Dev knew, one in Chairwoman Yance's own office. *This must be a trick.*

She glanced at the innkeeper, but the young woman slept on. She somehow managed to look tired in her sleep, as if she'd used up all of her energy long ago.

Taking a few sips of water from her canteen, Dev examined the Chairwoman's message again. It seemed recent. Had Yance been in contact with Netherby, even after he'd been reported missing? Why hadn't she gotten word to the lab?

Dev looked at the satchel from which she'd taken the escritoire, Netherby's initials clearly stamped there too. *The man loved to put his mark on things.* She tried to recall more about how she had come by the bag, but her mind flinched from the subject. She wanted nothing more than the safety of her small, lonely room at the Ironford boardinghouse right then. Or, barring that, the uncomfortable bed at the Deaf King. Her whole body ached. She was as tired as the innkeeper, and no wonder. She'd slept on the ground. Beside an ancient sewer. Near an innkeeper who knew more about the gems, and the palace, than she let on. Dev's eyes narrowed at Lurai. Was it Lurai who had tricked her? Had her mother done the same to Netherby?

No. Whatever the innkeepers had been searching for, Dev knew what Netherby was capable of. The trickery had his marks all over it.

Glancing at the dark tunnel, Dev tried to remember what she could. Lurai had brought her here. It had smelled like a sewer.

But where had she found Netherby's bag and escritoire?

As she prodded her memories, they only fragmented further. Netherby's bag, the dusty tunnel. Sunlight, impossibly far below the ground. Something red. Whispers: *Release me.*

Shivering, Dev tried to stand. As she braced her hands on the ground to steady herself, she noticed her fingers. Pieces of gleaming silver wire like what Lurai wore were wrapped around both index fingers and her thumbs. She touched her pinched ears. More wire.

Meanwhile, the innkeeper's wire wrappings were missing. "Lurai, what did you do?"

The innkeeper cracked an eye open, and looked at Dev. She still had a small silver curl on each ear, but the decorations were much less elaborate than before.

"I protected you," she said, drowsily. Her voice sounded thick.

Dev turned her head one way and the next. *I heard bees in the tunnel, I think. A buzz or hum echoing.* The hum was definitely gone, though her head still ached. She looked around. The sun had begun to set. She was free to go back to the dig, or back to the Deaf King. Or back on the train and as far from here, and these people, as possible.

She couldn't decide which would be safer. *I have to warn—*

Whom? Dev wasn't sure. *And about what?* She didn't know that either.

She returned the escritoire and her own satchel to Netherby's bag. "We have to tell the dig master. He'll want to know about the tunnel." Once she told Lannert, she could go home.

Lurai said nothing for a long time. Then finally, she spoke, her voice cracking. "You are certain that you didn't see anyone in the tunnel? Or beyond that?"

"I . . ." Dev felt panic. Had she seen someone? Maybe? But definitely not Lurai's mother. *Whatever I saw, I never want to see again. I need to get out of here, away from this place.* She shook her head slowly. No, she could not leave without finding her grandmother's page, or Netherby. That had been her entire goal. But even so, her entire being was leaning in the direction of *AWAY*.

Go home, her heart battered to her ribs. *Home home home.* "I don't . . . I need to go—"

Lurai watched her, eyes narrowing, but Dev's mind was racing along the path that her family had taken when they'd left the valley. *Where is home, really? The Far Reaches? My gran is gone. My mother too. Ironford? My life there was my work. A life Netherby stole and brought here.* She'd brought more belongings with her to the Jeweled Valley than she'd left in the Ironford boardinghouse. Yet she wanted to leave nonetheless. She grasped the handle of her mentor's bag and tried to force just one more memory about where she'd found it.

Her mind filled with color: rust red. She recoiled.

"We must go, Lurai, and fast." *Away from this place.* She had proof of Netherby's last known whereabouts now, even if she didn't know how she'd come by it. She would bring this to the Symposium. She would run the dust of the tunnel through the micrograph if she had to. To be able to say, *All I could find of him in the dig was this bag, which contains gemstone residue consistent with . . .* something scientific sounding. Perhaps that would be sufficient to at least close the Society's inquiry?

Lurai rose and brushed herself off. "I understand. I'd hoped for more." The words were mumbled, disappointed. She'd been looking for her mother. Dev knew how horrible that felt. But she could not help further. She'd caused enough commotion in the Idary family as it was. She would leave before worse happened.

"I will need to leave the inn immediately. I'll just get my bags," she said, turning in the direction she thought would take her back up the hill. "I must go home and examine my data there." She walked forward, thinking of her tools, at the inn. With her free hand, she began to pry the silver wires loose from her ears.

For a moment, the meadow swayed dizzyingly, but then it righted itself again. She lifted her fingers from the wires and the ground steadied.

"And you." Dev tugged at Lurai's arm. "Your guests will be needing you." It was nearly dark. Perhaps they would get back to the Deaf King before supper and avoid another scandal.

Lurai walked by her side, unusually compliant. She seemed to be listening for something. Or *to* something. "You must keep the bands on until you are clear of the valley, cousin. They will keep you safe."

Cousin. "How much do you know about my family?" Dev finally said. Did they know that her grandmother had had the lapis page, that she'd given it to Dev? *That I lost it?* She pressed her fingers against her chest, where the pendant usually hung.

"Know? What's there to know? Your family left the valley, as many did. Why?"

Dev didn't press. She bit her lip as they emerged from the

woods, a much farther walk than she remembered, climbed the hill, and made their way past the dig entrance. The tents were quiet. No lamps glowed. No sounds of shovel against earth echoed. Dev blinked at the sight of the tent flaps, tied shut. Matthais and Vandina were nowhere to be seen. Nor Lannert. The dig had paused for dinner. She and Lurai kept walking, dust billowing in their wake.

The climb back up to the Deaf King was beyond difficult. For Dev, each step fell heavier than the last. The innkeeper, too, was nearly silent, almost sleepwalking. The ground below the two women's feet seemed to shake and sway.

When they reached the cobwebbed porch, Dev's chest rattled as if it was empty and she'd left her soul in the tunnel. But that was ridiculous. Instead of brushing the remaining dust from her clothing before entering, she removed her coat and flipped it inside out, trapping the evidence inside.

She heard the escritoire tick again. By now she could imagine the message: *Release*—No. That wasn't right. *Report.*

She could reply, Dev realized. Tell the Society what she'd found. *As Netherby, perhaps? Since I have his escritoire.* But what had she discovered? Her memories kept surfacing, then sinking away, still splintered and hazy. Her head ached to think too hard about it. And Lurai leaned against her as if she was about to topple over.

Dev nearly jumped out of her skin when the kitchen door burst open.

"Where have you been?" Lurai's grandmother rushed to them. "You've nearly missed supper."

"We were exploring." Lurai yawned. "The dig."

"Did you not feel the quake then? Were you hurt?" She

stared at them as if they might disappear again. "Everyone fled the dig and said they hadn't seen you. They're in the great room still. You should see to your guests, Lurai."

"Seismic trouble?" Dev hadn't felt a thing. "We must have fallen during the quake."

"You are both very lucky," Lurai's grandmother scolded. "How could you make me worry, Lurai? After what happened to your mother."

Lurai's face crumpled. "I didn't mean to worry you; I heard—I thought I heard someone. But we didn't find—"

"Best get washed up and ready to work. You look half ghost." She frowned at her grandchild, then glared at Dev. "She's needed far too much to make up for her mother's absence. You cannot take her away from me too."

"I am sorry. It is entirely my fault." Dev felt dizzy with déjà vu. Lurai had said she'd heard voices before. *I will think on that later.* "I lost track of time. I'll pay double your rate on the room and make good on any more of Netherby's debts as well."

She didn't have even a quarter of that money left. She was making promises on air. She fully intended to be headed back to Ironford, and away from these people, cousins or not.

But the old woman's face eased, and she nodded assent. "Be sure it doesn't happen again. Lurai stays here. Your supper is on the table." She gestured toward the hearth, where the two Far Reaches academics sat, their robes clean and brushed. A steaming bowl rested on the table between them.

Dev hesitated. Her former colleagues would want to know where she'd been, and what she'd found. A memory from the tunnel appeared, jagged and glittering in her mind, then disappeared. Suddenly the last thing she wanted was to eat, especially not in the great room.

Too late. Vandina spotted her and waved her over. "Dev! We hope you'll join us!"

Matthais's eyes took in the bag she carried. "Those are Netherby's initials! Did you find it in the woods or something? You've got brambles in your hair. Tell us what happened!"

Dev's hand went to her braid. Sure enough, she'd brought a good cross section of the forest back with her.

Vandina leaned in and whispered, "Did you find the innkeeper too? The mother, I mean?"

Dev shook her head. "We didn't find anyone. Just the bag." *That was right, wasn't it?*

"Well, let's look at it!" Matthais reached for it, but Dev swatted his hand away.

"The Society must know of it first. I'm under instructions to send word back to them immediately."

"Oh come now, Dev. That will take hours. Tell us at least where you found the thing," Matthais persisted.

But Vandina prodded him. "Leave her be to eat at least." The scholar held out a buttered roll. "We thought we might go back to the dig tonight. Our source says they might find more of the court soon."

Dev held the roll so tightly, her fingertips sank deep. She tried to take a bite, to buy herself time, but chewing made her feel ill. The roll tasted like dust. *Like the tunnel.*

She chewed and chewed, finally swallowing hard. Dev knew she couldn't tell them about the tunnel, or anything else.

Matthais looked once more at the satchel. "Imagine. All this time, he'd just left it in the woods. What do you think happened? We must mount an investigation. Get our own teams into the dig. And then we'll all go back to Ironford together. This will be a very interesting Symposium indeed." He rose and pulled out a chair for her. Dev swallowed again, the bread sticking to her throat.

The last thing she wanted was to have the scholars' help investigating.

Without wanting to, one knee, then the other buckled slowly and she took her seat, although not among equals. Her good and now muddied lab coat was piled in her lap. The dusty edges of her canvas skirts were pale beside the broad, vibrant hems of their Society robes.

Never had she felt so much lesser than someone else.

"What do I think happened? I didn't find Netherby. That's what happened," she said. "And I don't want to look anymore. I just want to go home." Something felt wrong about that statement. Like it was not quite a fib. Had she found him? Hadn't she? She had his bag. Something was keeping her from remembering. She smelled copper and heard a buzzing sound. Bile rose in her throat.

"We figured the bag would wash up by the river, having been pitched off the fourth bridge! The dig master had threatened to do that to Netherby." Matthais laughed, but his eyes narrowed. "Are you certain you didn't find anything else?"

Vandina relented, patting her hand. "Quiet, Matthais! Now that she's found his bag, the Society will celebrate her, and send us funds to find more. Always hungry for more information and discoveries, aren't they? It's like rowing against a tide, trying to keep the Society satisfied. But you must be patient."

Dev nodded, playing along, hoping to be able to make an escape soon. "I had hoped to find more—something about the Book of Gems—a legendary prince. . . ." The buzzing in her ears made her vague and thoughtless. She'd nearly said she'd hoped to recover her own research. Had she done that? Netherby's bag felt heavy enough for that.

Vandina smiled sympathetically. "What if we submitted a proposal to keep you on at the dig indefinitely? You could send the bag back with the next shipment and we'll tell Lannert you're essential here. You could continue to work evenings on the book, gather your 'prince' stories while you work with us the rest of the time? We could join forces for the Symposium. Maybe we'll be among the first to see the heart of the fortress."

Essential. She'd never been that. Dev imagined long discussions over endless pots of tea and lemon pastries. It sounded desperately normal. She leaned toward them. Then the escritoire ticked and she cleared her throat to cover the noise.

Release me. Or *Report.* Which message would it be now?

"And afterward," Vandina continued, "we could publish something together. Bring you into the fold the right way? We had wondered why you didn't do so with Netherby. But then we met him. You would do well to find other mentors."

Vandina smiled broadly. They were the same age. And yet Vandina was proposing to take her on as an assistant. What would that be like? No worse than what she'd already done. But Dev didn't want to do it. And she wouldn't show them the valise. Nor anything else.

Go home, her heart said. Or the beat of something very much like her heart. *Release me.*

Dev startled. She had to get out of the great room. "It is a generous offer. I hope you'll give me time to consider it."

To her surprise, Vandina didn't look upset. "You do good work, Dev. And you came to find your mentor, despite everything. Anyone would be lucky to have you in their lab. And as a colleague at the Society. Take all the time you need. We'll see you at the dig? Or what's left of it after today's rumbles."

The scientists turned back to their unfinished meal. Only then did Dev realize what they'd been eating: a thick mash of oats with honey. A supper much like what her grandmother used to make when she was feeling ill.

Even more unsettled, Dev rose from the table and hurried down the hall to her room to pack and to think. If she could escape from here—where would she go?

She fumbled with her key, lost in thoughts about the tunnel and her own trail of broken memories. About the shape of her future if she didn't return to the dig, nor to Ironford. More and more she wanted to run, not return.

She unlocked the door and was struck once more by a cold breeze. The window, open again.

Then she stopped moving, her breath stilled in her chest.

Her room looked like it had been turned upside down and shaken. The quilt lay across the floor, the sheets piled at the edge of the bed with scraps of paper—Netherby's messages—stuck upright in the folds. With a lurching sense of doom, Dev pulled the mattress up. The space below was empty. The lapis pendant, which she'd removed rather than risk anyone spotting it at the dig, was gone, along with the data, and the micrograph. The Society's dossier also.

Her research! Her tools! Everything. The last piece of the lapis page. This was beyond a childish prank. This was theft, pure and simple.

Only Netherby's bag, which she'd kept by her knee at the table, remained. His escritoire nestled inside, silent, for once. Dev shuddered. She had little now to return to the Society with. No Netherby, no new data. *Nothing.*

The innkeeper had warned her. Chairwoman Yance had forbidden her to travel. And Dev knew she had only herself to blame. Everyone else would see it that way too. She barely had time to think about the losses before the escritoire began ticking again. A new message. She reached inside the valise.

Her satchel had slipped down the side of Netherby's bag and was stuck. Dev's heart skipped. Her fingers touched fabric, then something cool and slick. *Like Gran's lapis, before Netherby broke it.* She sighed with relief. She'd put it in her bag, hadn't she? She hadn't left it in her room. This was one good thing in a jumble of bad things.

Excitedly, she knelt in her wrecked room to lift the artifact shard from the bag.

But nestled among frayed and filthy clothing and jammed against the escritoire was much more than a piece of a lapis page.

She pulled out a thick, silver-bound book made of lapis lazuli.

No.

Inscribed in gems of all colors across the cover, in ancient valley script: *The Book of Gems, a Catalog of the Jeweled Valley Treasury.* And as Dev watched, a tendril of silver ink curled along the edge of the title and wrote, still in valley script: *The Prince of Gems.*

Dev stuffed the book back in the bag. *I'm hallucinating. This isn't happening.*

The cold breeze blew over her disheveled, emptied room.

She looked at the satchel again, knowing the reason it had felt so heavy as she dragged it up the hillside.

Netherby, you utter ass.

The Esteemed Scientist had attempted to steal the Book of Gems.

She stared at the rag-cushioned lapis pages, at the gems glittering on the cover, a few freed from their bezels and now sparkling in the corners of the satchel. The Jeweled Valley's most ancient treasure.

Here, with me.

Netherby had tried to take it home nestled beneath his dirty laundry.

He hadn't run away. He hadn't been hiding. He'd been trying to steal the original, mythical book from its rightful owners. From the fortress. *And what has happened to him?* Dev couldn't remember much beyond shadows near the bag. Something glittering, viridian, perhaps—

No. No. Dev shook her head, forcing herself to think clearly. That had been inside the tunnel, beneath the fortress. She tasted the grit of the tunnel in her teeth.

Then she groaned, realizing the truth.

Netherby hadn't stolen the Book of Gems.

I stole it. Me.

She'd removed the bag and the book from the fortress dig.

She was in so much trouble. With Lannert. With the Society. With everyone in the Jeweled Valley. *I must undo this.*

Dev stumbled back into the hallway, from her freezing-cold room, gripping the valise so tightly, her fingers felt welded to the handle.

As her door blew shut from the wind, the innkeeper's grandmother shouted from a room down the hall, "Lurai! Lurai? Oh, gems help us."

8.

THE GEMS SPEAK SO LOUDLY NOW, *but I can hear you, Gran.* Lurai felt tears prickle her eyes as her grandmother shook her by the shoulder, trying to get her to speak.

Lurai didn't want to disobey her grandmother, but it hurt too much to talk. Her tongue felt hard and sharp. Her jaw ached. *What is happening to me?* The gems hummed and buzzed, singing to her, drowning out her grandmother's cajoling words. Then Dev burst in, and her eyes went to the pile of belongings at Lurai's side. The bench tools. The unbound pendant shard held fast in Lurai's grip.

"I'm so sorry, Doctor," Lurai's grandmother said. "I never thought she could do such a thing."

"Did you take the rest of my things tonight as well?" Dev asked. Lurai shook her head slowly. She held out the tools. She'd been trying to listen, just as Calia had. Just as her mother had, once, going through the scholars' things, searching for clues to the dig.

And then—oh then, her mother's skin had become mottled, and a sapphire pushed through her skin at her collarbone. She'd been so afraid. But Netherby had said he could fix it.

And then she was gone.

"Lurai?" Her grandmother's fingers dug into her arm. Her cloudy eyes searched Lurai's, looking for answers.

Lurai could no longer give her grandmother the answers she sought. This was her fault, her choice. She'd removed her wards in order to save Dev. *Now I am becoming the answer.*

"I'm so sorry." Gran turned to Dev. "We're both very sorry, aren't we, Lurai? She's been in a daze since you returned. And you said she may have hit her head in the quake?"

Dev spoke, but Lurai heard it as if listening through a haze; she could barely make out "she tried to help me." The gems were so loud in her head, but she managed a nod. She'd needed to help, so that Dev could help them all. That's what the gems wanted too.

"Answer me. Apologize to the doctor." Her grandmother swatted her shoulder. Then she peered closer, her dim eyes squinting, as she tucked Lurai's long hair behind an ear. "Where are your rings and bindings?"

Gran was shouting again. At Lurai. At Dev. Who wore Lurai's glittering bindings clearly visible on one ear now.

"Thief!" Gran shrieked.

"No, she wrapped them on me—I never asked for them," Dev countered. "Lurai, tell her." Dev began to pull the bindings from her fingers.

"It's true." Lurai painfully opened her mouth—to protest and defend Dev. *This is my doing; she was only trying to help,* she wanted to say. But at the sight of Lurai's tongue, Gran shrieked. "No, not again. No." The older woman collapsed, weeping.

What has happened to me? Lurai lifted her fingers to her

mouth. Touched something hard.

"Oh." Dev's mouth formed an oval of shock. She stared just like Gran had. "Your tongue. It's covered with moonstone."

Lurai shivered. She'd already known the truth, but hearing it just made things feel worse.

"This is what happened to your mother?" Dev asked. Without waiting for a reply, she knelt to check on Gran. "She will be okay. Her pulse is strong." Then she came and sat by Lurai and held her hand.

This is because I asked you to go into the tunnel, instead of going myself. This is because I tried to protect you—I did protect you—from this fate. The bands will keep you safe. You must not take them off. Lurai stared at Dev, willing her to understand. Her mother had once done the same for her, with her own wire wrappings.

"Lurai, you took my things because you are still trying to protect me?"

Lurai nodded, but her eyes drooped. She watched as Dev blinked hard, listening.

She could hear the gems telling Dev a story. Reminding Dev of red, clustered gems, near a body. Near the valise.

"Is it the valise and what's inside that's causing these changes? Did you touch anything in the bag while I slept?"

Lurai nodded again. She'd needed to see if her mother had left any other messages. Her fingers had brushed against the gems that had fallen from their bindings. And then she'd heard them sing. She'd heard the Prince's voice.

Worse, *Dev* had certainly touched both book and escritoire as well. Would the same thing happen to her?

The doctor gasped as if she had the same thought. "I have to find help," she whispered. *"But where? I have to take the book back. Now. I must talk to—to whom? To Lannert? No."*

Was the doctor speaking or thinking? Lurai couldn't tell. She could hear Dev clearly now. Just like Netherby.

Dev tilted her head, as if listening. "Netherby could still speak when I saw him."

Yes, Cousin, in the glittering dark, Lurai agreed. She looked at her grandmother. Wished she could hug the woman, or Calia, one more time.

Calia. If no one protects her, she could be next. Turned to gems. Lurai had to do something.

Dev stood. "I must try to talk to Netherby. If he is still breathing."

Lurai nodded emphatically. *He will definitely understand what is happening. But you must take me with you.*

Dev jotted a note to Gran. She whispered, "I'm sorry, I'm sorry," and signed her name, and beneath that, *cousin.* Then she tried to slip out of the room alone. But Lurai stood and grabbed hold of the bag handle too. She began to pull, heading toward the door.

"You can't. You must stay here," Dev protested. "You're too sick."

Cousin, he calls, and the gems too, Lurai thought. *And we must heed.* Then she dragged Dev down the hallway into the Deaf King Inn's late-night silence, and pulled them both onto the dark trail as the ground began to rumble again. Together, they would bring the book back to the throne room. They would make this right again.

~

NEWTOWN, IRONFORD, ANN. ___15.

Society to Netherby: Please give location. Report ASAP.

9.

DEV AND LURAI STOOD OUTSIDE the stone-covered sewage drain of the ancient fortress. The moon had set and the sun had yet to peek over the hills.

Lurai held Dev's hand so tightly, she couldn't pull away. Along their tumbling run down the hillside, she'd finally convinced Lurai to let go. But only for as long as Dev was heading in the same direction as she. Now her grip was like a metal vise.

I can hear the Prince of Gems speaking.

Lurai had said that to her. And Dev had seen Netherby. Beneath a pile of stolen gems. *Is that what I'll become too?* If there was any way to save her cousin and herself from this fate, she would find it.

Struggling, Dev managed to wrest her hand from Lurai's. "I do this under my own power," she finally said, not certain who she addressed. Lurai didn't say a word as together they rolled the stone away from the tunnel. As they worked, Dev thought of what rested inside Netherby's bag: glittering blue pages of the legendary, and whole, Book of Gems. It was unthinkable.

You must not touch anything. You will be searched.

She kept an ear out for the dig master, or any guards who might catch them on their rounds past the fortress, but the campsite was silent. Lannert had said taking *anything* from the dig without permission was a crime punishable by expulsion from the valley.

And taking—the book? Dev couldn't imagine the infamy. It would mean the outright ruin of her career. Of course, they'd first have to make it out of the tunnel without turning into gems for Dev to even have a career left to be ruined.

Lurai grunted at her. The innkeeper's eyes were clear, but her cheeks glittered with veins the color of moonstone and jade. *Oh gods. Hurry.*

Dev's mind whirled. She did not want to reenter the tunnel. *I must return the book to the dungeon at least. Immediately. Perhaps that will keep Lurai from a worse fate.*

As she knelt by the entrance, Dev wobbled with fear and nausea. Her mouth filled with the taste of copper; her eyes swam with visions of garnets. Now she could clearly remember what had before been a blurry memory. Netherby's body, a pile of gemstones. Was Lurai next?

Out of all her failings, Dev realized, her impact on her cousin's life was the worst. Was Dev no better than Netherby? No. She would help Lurai. And then, perhaps, resolve her own problems too. *Otherwise, the Society will lock its doors to me forever once this is known. And I will deserve it.*

Dev swore she would return the book, force Netherby to help Lurai, and then leave the region altogether.

She would even renounce science if that would fix things. And give up on becoming a member of the Society. She stepped forward.

For the second time, Dev broke into the Jeweled Palace by way of a sewer.

Yes. She would put the book back. She would erase all evidence of her presence. Quickly. Before the next quake. And even if the seismic shifts near the fortress didn't cover up what she'd done, at the rate the dig was going the valley citizens wouldn't find the dungeon, much less the antechamber and Netherby's glittering body, for a decade. Dev could be long gone by then.

She crawled, and Lurai followed.

The walls began to hum. Dev stopped, dust boiling around them. She tried once again to peel off the silver wards, to give the innkeeper some protection.

Lurai shook her head, beckoning Dev to press on. She began to moan so terribly that Dev panicked and started crawling again, pushing the bag up the tunnel. "It's all right; it's going to be all right!" Dev shouted through the din. Lurai grew quiet again.

She thought of Lurai's determination. How much she'd wanted to help Dev.

Lurai had stripped off her own wards to protect Dev. Now Dev had to help Lurai.

Netherby's monogrammed bag was nearly impossible to move. It hadn't been this heavy earlier, had it?

The sides of it bulged, as if about to tear.

Dev managed to shove it through the end of the tunnel and up into the bone-filled anteroom. She remembered this now. She sat down to check on the book. When she opened the bag, she saw the book had increased in width, growing more pages from the center. Several of the lapis leaves had already fallen away from the main spine. Just like in the hall—she remembered now. The light-filled room with the stand and the—

Dev sat down in the chamber and stared at the book. As she watched, a page grew from the center of the spine, and a strange, curling writing began to appear on it.

Spelled one word.

Her name.

Dev. Devdevdevdevdev.

"STOP THIS!" she yelled, feeling quite mad. She was yelling at a book. The thick dirt walls of the lower fortress echoed her words back to her.

I can hear the prince of gems speaking. That's one of the last things Lurai had said to her. And then she'd taken her wards off and given them to Dev. What was happening to Lurai now was because of that sacrifice.

She could almost hear the hum reply to her, but it was muffled. The rings, they protected her. Lurai had said that too.

She looked at the innkeeper. Her eyes were closed. She swayed to the hum.

Meantime, the writing didn't stop. The script changed. It grew bolder and more ornate, and rushed to fill the page.

"Listen, I don't know how you are doing this," Dev began. "Netherby, if this is you trying to scare me away, or to cover up a worse crime, stop it now. You need to help Lurai."

The Prince of Gems speaks, the ruby-colored inscriptions curled across the blank page.

"There is no prince of gems," Dev replied, wincing at the sound of her voice in the cave. "That's a story for children." Unlucky, Lurai had said.

I am bound here against my will. The words were eerily similar to the messages Dev had discovered stuck in the escritoire.

To the ghost story Lurai had begun telling, then stopped. Of course Netherby would have heard the stories. Dev remembered those selfsame words coming from her mouth in the laboratory when she'd tried to micrograph the page. *Release me and I will help the girl. And you.*

Lurai's eyes widened at the writing, although it did not seem to make sense to her.

"This is just another of his terrible tricks," Dev assured the innkeeper. Netherby, in the other room, must have figured out how to make the book transfer messages. She remembered his eyes following hers. Why would he do this?

And yet. She recalled the strange message segments. The syntax that seemed so very out of date, and in old Lapidarian.

She remembered her studies of the false emerald and her grandmother's stories of the time the world almost ended. Could someone have turned the book into an escritoire? She could not see how.

The writing scrolled down the margin of a page.

"I'm a scientist. This can't be real," Dev whispered. She would return the book to where it belonged. To the pedestal. She would get different, safer artifacts for the Society. Then she would find help for Lurai. Someone would know what to do for her in Ironford.

The tunnel shook. Or she shook and it felt like the tunnel.

This is real. You must free me. You must not put me back in the dungeon, the book wrote, before Dev's eyes, alongside a description of Carmelite Rosa bracelets.

"The dungeon?" She couldn't help herself. She was talking to the book. "We are already there."

The pedestal has a binding on it. Just like the book does. If left there, alone, I will eventually run out of ink. And without me, the valley will be overrun by gems, as will everyone who touches them. First, the valley. Then the Six Kingdoms. The gems have been waiting. I am the last thing that holds them back from the world.

"Do you mean to say that you and the book control the gems? That the Jeweled Court was at the gems' mercy until the book was made?"

Much more than that. The valley's gems and its Jewels were once one family. They still hunger for power. Unless we bind the gems, they'll master everything. And if the unbound gems escape beyond the valley, the Six Republics will fall.

Dev thought that would be far worse than what the emerald printing press had threatened to do. It also sounded like the dreams of a mad king. Just as Lurai had said?

The Book of Gems was ancient. If there was a prince of gems writing to her in the margins of the lapis pages, how old was he? And how mad?

As Dev read the writing in the book's margins, she began to hear the words in her bones. Like a whisper, not a hum. She could only imagine what it sounded like to Lurai without her wards.

"Netherby, tell me how you're really writing these messages," she demanded. "Before we go any further. It's an escritoire trick? Another fake?"

The tunnel shook again, but another page began growing from the center of the book. One of the farthest pages out began to pull lose. Dev had a hard time imagining how Netherby could ever manage something as complex as this.

When the ink returned, it was thinner and paler. Answering in this way was taxing whatever powered the book. Was that a way to escape? To run it dry? To save Lurai?

"I'll put you back where Netherby found you. Then I'll tell Lannert. The dig teams can get you out the proper way," she decided, hating the fact that she was already talking to the book as if it was a person.

But that feeling drained from her as new words appeared on the page. The book was listening to her too. This was not a trick.

That will be the end of the kingdom, the book replied. *And the gems will be turned loose on the world. All of them, at once.*

The dungeon's walls shook and cracked.

The newest gems want this more than I can say. They are wild. They've never been trained. They don't understand. The book is meant to help them understand their power, as much as it is to help the Jewels and lapidaries understand. And now—

Dev shut the bag tight, silencing the book. "No. No. No. This is not possible." She dragged the bag, and the book, toward the pedestal room—the room where Netherby lay. She could hear his escritoire ticking in her bag. Was that how he was controlling the book? Some link through the gems strewn over him to the escritoire and the book? It had to be.

She knew all too well that her mentor was capable of cruel trickery. Especially if he didn't want to be caught. But at this level?

She looked back at her companion. Lurai's lips had turned moonstone pale as she helped her push the valise. The bag had become so heavy, and so filled with pages, that they couldn't carry it. They made it to the final steps of the corridor and were nearly to the door when rocks clattered loud to the ground. A wave of dust poured toward them.

Dev covered her nose and mouth, then dove to cover Lurai also. When the dust cleared, their faces showed mostly clean, but the rest of the room, and part of Netherby, was brown with a layer of silt. Gems glittered dimly beneath.

Her breath echoed strangely in her ears. The pressure of the room had changed slightly. It felt somehow hollow in here now.

She knew then what that sound had been. The tunnel, collapsing. And perhaps part of the dungeon room as well.

They had to get out of there, and fast. With Netherby, if at all possible. He had so many things to answer for.

Dev looked at Netherby. His eyes had filmed over with dust.

The gems covered more of him now. Only a few fingers and those unblinking, dead eyes remained. He would not be answering anything.

"Hurry, we must get out of here, or we'll be crushed," Dev whispered. "Leave the book here." She pointed, but Lurai dragged the valise toward the skylight.

Struggling as the fortress rocked and shook, they climbed the rockfall out of the dungeon into the space above. A giant moonstone throne stood behind the hole. It gave off a faint white light, casting the large room in sharp shadows. And as Dev gazed around the enormous hall, squinting at cascades of earth pouring in through breaches in the walls, she could not see a single way out.

She was no longer a thief. Now she was a prisoner.

PART THREE

10.

Undated escritoire, no location received.

Netherby to Society: I have not betrayed you. I must not betray you. Those in power conspire to possess what is rightly yours and I will not conspire. I will share your words, I am studying your words, my Prince. That will not be a betrayal. I am not betraying you.

~

A battle raged inside Lurai. The gems—the moonstone coursing through her especially—wanted to destroy the book and bury the prince. The doctor too, if it came to that. The gems would be free, and the book stood in their way. Lurai's jaw stiffened. *Calia. Gran.* She would not help the gems.

She felt each page of the book scream as it cataloged and bound another gem. She felt the gems scream back. And still she strained against herself, to help Dev and her family. The whole valley. With each moment, the fight grew more difficult, as the gems made her body grow harder.

Nevertheless, I will fight you, she thought. Her teeth clenched around her moonstone tongue. *I will protect my valley and its people.*

If she could figure out how in time.

If she could convince Dev that the book was not one of Netherby's tricks. Which she had no way of doing.

Even as she fought it, Lurai felt more gems begin to rise through the earth. Another quake was coming. She could not stop them.

~

Dev knelt on the vast moonstone floor of the half-buried hall.

The archeo-gemologist in her knew that she trespassed on the ancient court of lapidaries and Jewels. Her grandmother's stories of the valley told her to be prepared for the gems to take her mind from her. Her muscles tensed as the earth continued to shake and she expected to be crushed at any minute by the enormous jade columns supporting the crumbling ceiling.

How long had this room withstood the pressures of the region's tectonics before it was released from the crevasse? Had the gems that lined the hall helped protect it? Dev guessed it must be so. But how?

A few days ago, she would have demanded to know the answers to these questions, and she knew the book beside her might tell her. But now? Now she needed to free her cousin from the gems. To help the people of the valley before it was too late. The walls shook as she searched the room for clues for how to stop the quakes and contain the gems.

The room refused to give up its secrets. Her cousin moaned.

"Lurai," she whispered, and the walls echoed her voice back, louder than she'd spoken. "We will make it out of here."

As if making a lie of her words, the ground shook again. The smell of raw earth from the far wall fought with the older, deeper tang of thick dust. Layers of spiderwebs blanketed the room. It smelled like a grave. Dev shivered. She refused to let it be theirs.

The combination of dust and webs formed an age-thick layer of gray obscuring most of the columns and many of the mosaics on the walls.

Dev brushed a finger along a seam between three different shades of red quartz, tracing an ancient alternating pattern: Gemstones, then people. Gems covering people. Then figures wrapping stones in wire. Then the book, bright blue against the red. The panel ended there. The next mosaic was all blues and greens—an ancient valley landscape: the river, the town, the valley. This landscape had no bridges or deep ravines. A palace stood brightly walled in the center of an open meadow. A pretty panel.

The book had saved the valley.

Now, the palace and the meadow had gone generations buried in different shifts of the earth over time. A mudslide here, a rumble there. The sinkhole that had swallowed much of the fortress and surrounding grounds had eventually filled in with earth and a silted pond. And the gems were breaking free because Netherby had found a way through the broken earth to the moonstone court, and had woken them. With a shudder, Dev realized that Netherby's destructive journey had begun just after she'd sent the lapis page of the Book of Gems through the micrograph. Netherby hadn't been the only person to wake the Jeweled Court. Dev looked at Lurai with even more guilt. Her cousin stared back, begging her to do something.

"What, though?" she asked the air.

The book rustled, another lapis page growing from its

spine. *You must place me on the throne, Dev.*

Netherby? She would never have been able to lift him, even before he turned to garnets. "How? The body is buried in the crevasse."

That was not a Prince. I am, the book replied. *None but me.*

Dev realized with a jolt that the interruptions to Netherby's early escritoires had not been Netherby.

"You've been trying to talk to us? For how long?" She marveled at the book. "Didn't you realize the Society would want to steal you and put you on display?" Dev stared at the book. "Where you could infect more people . . ."

Not infect. I want to protect. With the palace revealed, it was only a matter of time.

Dev frowned. "The Society only wants to protect. To bring knowledge forward."

It wants to possess.

"So you would have been transported to Ironford, or the Far Reaches, away from the throne."

Or with the throne.

As she read the words, Dev knew the truth. The Society wanted to control and profit from everything here. They would risk everything to do it.

And I wanted to help them.

"Then what happens to the valley? To Lurai and her family?"

If the book and the throne leave the valley, the gems will follow them.

Dev blinked salt and dust out of her eyes, and Lurai blinked too. "That would mean disaster for the Six Republics, as well as the valley. I won't let it happen."

The dig would not make it to the moonstone court before Dev starved and Lurai turned to moonstone. But once people did arrive, the pieces of the throne room would likely be sold off in secret—despite the rules—doled out among the museums of the Six Republics by the Society. Researchers would write papers and give presentations, lending legitimacy to the Society, all the while enabling it to steal more history.

What the Society allowed to stay in the valley would only be a small portion of the former palace. The beautiful artifacts Dev could see: glittering columns, ancient inscriptions. Elegant inlays. All of it would certainly go.

And the gems would follow. Dev blinked away visions of people encrusted with garnets.

The enormous throne waited cold and still beneath its own layer of dust. It was so big it could easily seat two. Dev moved closer and wiped away the dust from one armrest: the gold-chased, ancient word for *Jewel* came clean. On the other armrest, a rough gash in the stone revealed a space where a longer word had been, but it was now a decorative pattern of lapis and tourmaline.

Long ago, the prince wrote, *that read* lapidary. *They ruled together. They helped control the gems. But no longer. Unless you place the book on the throne.*

The ground rumbled and Lurai groaned again. Dev realized with a burst of adrenaline that she did not wish to die. Not here, not *anywhere*. She wouldn't. And neither would Lurai.

She grasped her cousin's cold, hard hand. The ground shook. The leather bag toppled over without anyone touching it. Lapis pages spilled onto the dusty floor.

You must set me on the throne. The prince's tiny lettering appeared down the side of a description for the Celestine Caskets—a group of star-strung onyx baguettes. The command was so strong, Lurai lurched for the book and tried to shut it. But she was too weak. Dev moved to help her. But she stopped them both when another page grew from the center of the book. At first it was blank; then the gem-ink began making a catalog of the new gems nearby, trying to bind them. "How are you talking to me and doing that at the same time?" Dev demanded.

Lurai's mother, the book replied. *She is helping. We are working together. Work with us. Set the book on the throne.*

The book—the prince—could lie. Dev knew that. It could cure Lurai. Dev knew that also. If it didn't destroy itself, by writing. The names of gems had almost reached the end of the page. Another edge tore loose from the outer bindings.

Dev knew of no science that could make lapis pages grow. This was magic.

Lurai, watching beside her, reached a finger out to the book. "Muh," she whispered.

Mother. "You can hear her?"

Lurai blinked hard. A yes.

Lurai Idary, Dev realized. A piece of the mystery fell into place. *Idary. Their last name. Lapidary. How else could they hear each other? You know it's true. The valley runs in your veins too.*

Lurai crawled forward, reaching fingers toward the pages. Dev pushed the book away from her. She didn't want her to disappear into the book as well.

"If we do what you ask?" Dev finally whispered. "You'll help us? Will you help her? Not like her mother, or Netherby—"

Netherby, the book wrote quickly, *betrayed me—was trying to take the book out of the valley. He paid for his treachery. He is still paying.*

"No, he's not. He's dead." Dev shuddered. At least, she hoped Netherby was dead down there. Meantime, she had to advocate for herself and for Lurai. "We brought the book back. Where is Lurai's mother?"

She is here in the book, with me, wrote the prince. *It was the only way. Put me on the throne and you will be with her again. She is a lapidary. Like the young woman before you. Like you.*

Dev had to wrap her arms around the book and fight Lurai off in order to keep her from doing as the prince asked right away.

"I am no lapidary. And if what you say is true, prove it. Lurai's mother has not spoken. You are the only voice telling us this," she finally said. Lurai blinked and sat down, waiting.

The book was silent for a long time. Then, a curling script hesitantly began scratching out a few letters: *H A N N E.*

Lurai stood and pointed, wordlessly.

"Your mother's name," Dev guessed. Was it enough? She fought with her doubts. The book was wasting valuable ink trying to win her over, and now it had coughed up Lurai's mother's name. She turned to it. "You will not make Lurai part of the book too."

NO, the book wrote emphatically as the walls and floor shook again. *She will live.*

The quake did not cease. The floor began to crack. And the book, rocking with the emphasis of its own declarations, tilted into the crack. The ground rolled and the fissure widened, taking the book with it, until the thick pages stuck against a rough jut in the earth and stayed there.

Lurai watched the book fall and lunged for it. Her fingers, thick and slow with moonstone, missed. Dev knelt beside her, reaching, nearly falling in herself as the ground continued to shake. Lurai suddenly arched her body over Dev's, blocking falling dirt. Before the tremors ceased, another portion of the wall collapsed with a crash, just behind the throne.

They will not stop. They will break free. Dev knew it was true—the moonstone that was consuming her cousin pulsed with the gems' desire. What previous centuries of geological shifts began long ago these latest quakes would complete.

The moonstone court was shrinking, quake by quake.

The throne itself teetered over the crack where the Book of Gems stuck fast.

Dev couldn't see the bottom of the crevice. Where Netherby had rested, the floor below had fallen through. If the book fell farther it would be lost forever. But Lurai could not reach it.

Along the edge of the new fissure, large gemstones glittered. Colors dazzled but defied description. Reds and purples shone so dark as to seem almost black.

"What are those?" Dev whispered, entranced. But Lurai shook her, breaking their hold on her cousin. These were new gems. Strong ones. Dev could hear them whispering, *Destruction to the throne and the bindings.*

Dev couldn't trust the book, or the prince, and the new gems were trying to sway her. Lurai shuddered. Dev didn't trust anyone. But her arms were longer than Lurai's. *Can I reach it in time?* Dev heard the prince's voice, calling to her: *We will die. You must help us!*

Dev felt Lurai's gem-encrusted hand tighten on her own, as if begging her to understand.

~

Hear us!

Dev stared at the book, then the throne, looking for the source of the sound.

Her hand, caught in her cousin's grasp, was turning pale from loss of blood.

Help us!

The ground shook again and, down in the fissure, the book teetered. She would have to lean out over the quake-torn earth to grasp it, without touching any of the new gems. But she could hear them now—the words, the voices. And down in the pit, the open book wrote and wrote, calling for help as pages fell. Dev could hear it clearly.

With her cousin's stone grip as her anchor, Dev leaned into the fissure. Her fingers grasped a page, which began to loosen in the bindings. "Hold tight," she whispered. She reached farther, levering her whole body out over the hole, her arm straining painfully in Lurai's grasp. And she gathered the book up, holding tight to the binding itself. The words burned her fingers and she heard them hum: *Help us. Make us whole.* "Pull me back up," she whispered, and felt Lurai slowly, painfully, inch backward. Dev tightened her arm to her chest, cradling the book away from the new gems. By the time Lurai had pulled Dev and the book back onto the more solid tiles of the moonstone court, the words had begun to sound like a young man's voice in Dev's head.

"My Prince," she whispered, feeling the pull of the voice. Then she fought back, shouting, "Stop that! I do not permit it." She sat up and slammed the book shut, harder than any scientist or Society member would dare.

The humming stopped. Beside her, Lurai sat still, immobilized, with moonstone creeping toward her eyes.

"Is this what you did to Netherby?" Dev raged at the lapis book. "You will stay out of my head. You will free my cousin."

Lurai stared at Dev's hands on the book, frozen. "Muh," she whispered again.

Dev opened the book again, near the center. As she spread the pages, writing curled down the edge of a new entry on Markanian Voluptites: *A rare gold-infused gem with the power of compulsion.*

She didn't need to translate the Lapidarian any longer. She could read it as if it was her mother tongue. Maybe at one time, it had been.

Don't shut the book again. Unlike the new gems, I will not address you without permission. But know that if you do not act quickly, the valley will end, and everything with it, when the book ends. When I end. The gems will destroy everything. Freeing me allows the book to become what it once was. What you knew it to be. A record. Not a prison. And for me and Lurai's mother to become the next Jewel and lapidary. Lurai may become our embodiment, if she wishes. It has been done before—

"I am a scientist. Talking to a book. Arguing with gems." Dev wanted to throw the pages back in the fissure.

We will be the first Jewel of the era, Dev. You will be a hero to the world. A power among the Six Republics. It's what must hap-

pen. I do not know what else I can say to convince you.

Was the Prince pleading?

"I am listening." Dev's fingers, where she held the book, tingled. She hoped the bindings on her ears and fingers would continue to protect her from Netherby's fate, but she knew she was weakening.

The moonstone throne was meant to be mine, the book wrote. *When my blood turned to rubies, I became so much more capable of guiding the valley, and that throne was built to help. But the villagers imprisoned me here. In the book.*

The prince, the bad-luck one. With blood turned to gems. Had he gone mad, like Netherby? She turned toward the throne, and the earth shook again. This time, a jade pillar toppled, smashing down between her and the moonstone seat. The gems themselves were trying to keep her from putting the book on the throne.

"No!" Dev's voice rang out in the collapsing hall. She climbed over the pillar, Lurai slowly following.

The throne remained whole, although covered with dust and dirt. Dev brushed a hand over it. The seat was definitely meant for two people. A place from which Valley Jewels and their lapidaries had ruled for generations.

In the hum that echoed throughout the hall, she heard the ancient vows: *A lapidary must protect the Jewel; the Jewel must protect the valley and its people.* Dev clutched the book and the Prince bound within it.

Was that right? In her hands, the book grew warm, then cold. Writing appeared once more on the blue surface: *Lapidary, heed.*

The valley shook beneath the palace, harder still, as another page dropped away from the book.

Another pile of earth fell to the floor, but this time Dev heard the clatter of shovels. An indistinct shout. The dig had found them.

They are coming for us, not you. They wish to possess us.

But there was something else. "The valley's tremors..." She hesitated. "Those happen when the book's pages are falling away."

Yes. As the book grows weaker, the gems grow stronger. Hurry, Dev.

Dev remembered her pendant. She recalled the writing on the page, before Netherby had broken it:

A lapidary must rule the—

Was that right? No, Dev's finger brushed the edge of the throne. She spoke the words of her grandmother's page aloud: "A lapidary must *protect* the valley."

Dev placed the book on the throne. She heard Lurai sigh. But nothing else happened. "What now?"

Free me. Unbind me.

But as Lurai reached for the first bindings, a pickaxe broke through the dirt, causing a cascade of rocks and gems to the court floor.

"It's here! We've found it!" Matthais Oen's voice was triumphant. Then, surprised. "Dev!"

"We're here!" Dev cried. "But don't come any closer! It's too dangerous." Still, to hear another's voice after all this time made her heart skip with relief.

That joy quickly died when a wall cracked, stone fell away, and Matthais crawled into the throne room, followed by Vandina.

"We found you!" Matthais's celebration quieted as he took in the moonstone court, the young woman perched by the throne, and the Book of Gems on the throne. "And Dev. What have you found *us*?"

"I told you she was keeping things from us." Vandina raised her eyebrows at the book. "And such things. We will be heroes of the Six Republics."

Her voice echoed in the silent room. Then the pages of the Book of Gems rustled. Dev pressed a silver-bound hand to its cover. And Matthais leapt for the lapis book, hands unprotected.

"Stop!" Dev cried, pushing him away. "You must not."

"Dev, you have nothing to fear. We will give you full credit for your discoveries." Matthais tried to soothe her, even as he stared at Lurai. "But we must get you out of here, and your find, before the diggers come. They are aware that some are trapped, I'm sure, and will be working furiously to rescue us. Or at least the innkeeper."

Matthais smiled at Lurai with all his teeth. "How beautiful." His cloak was dusty and muddied, and the creases beside his eyes were lined with grime, but his scholar's braid and his wire-rimmed glasses gleamed in the dim light.

Lurai did look beautiful. She glowed, but it was the moonstone beneath her skin, not the light. It was still killing her. Matthais had to see that. The scholar paused, eyes squinting.

"The book, give it to me," Vandina reached past Matthais, her voice reverent. "I must see it with my own eyes."

"You cannot touch it without protection," Dev protested as she pivoted to block them from book and throne. "It, and everything else here, is too dangerous. Too active."

"Active? Nonsense, the Jewels handled the gems daily. You yourself have done so, obviously. And valley residents do all the time. Besides, these gems are ancient."

"None of your gems from the dig are real," Dev said, her suspicions finally realized. "You can run them through a micrograph if you don't believe me. But not now. I can touch the book because the bindings protect me." She gestured at her hands—the one holding the book and the one in her cousin's grasp.

"Dev. How utterly unprofessional," Vandina said. "I can't believe I offered you a collaboration." Both scientists looked shocked in the exact same way, as if they'd practiced it. Matthais moved closer. "Why are you trying to keep us from this discovery?"

"Don't—" Dev began, but Matthais grasped the book before she could stop him, almost ripping its cover from the fragile bindings. The valley floor shook so hard a ceiling beam fell, nearly crushing Lurai.

"Stop!" Dev wrestled for the book with Matthais while the Prince shook the ground. Neither one listened to her.

"It's ours," Matthais said. "We need the book. The Society must have the data and the magic." He lunged away from Dev, trying to run from the throne and the room with the book. She gripped harder, and Lurai slowly moved to her side.

As everyone pulled at the scientist, another chunk of the carved ceiling tumbled down and nearly crushed them. Pale, Matthais finally released the book, and Lurai scrambled to pick it up.

"It's not yours to demand!" Dev's voice shook above the hum and rumbling of the moonstone court. "The valley isn't a find! It's a place and a people."

"You can't expect me to give up the premier discovery in my life's work!" Matthais shouted. "That would ruin you too. All scholars would be ruined by this capitulation."

"Not all," Lurai said, without moving her lips. She held the book and watched them through eyes the color of the moon. "If you have the support of the Book of Gems, you will be permitted to read it. I have done so. And you do not have it. Yet."

Dev drew a tight breath. Her cousin speaking for the Prince meant the moonstone had run all through her. They had to act fast.

Matthais and Vandina glared at the two of them. "You cannot expect us to believe that."

As the ground rumbled beneath their feet, Dev wrapped her arm around her cousin's waist and began to pull her forward, toward the throne.

~

Lurai imagined she felt the book's beating heart pounding against her own chest, not Dev's. Would the Prince do what he'd promised once he attained the throne? She leaned against Dev to steady herself, as Matthais grabbed her around the waist.

They kept moving, but too slowly. *The throne. It is in reach, if only Matthais would let go.* The man's fingers were already turning opal white with the effort.

"Matthais." Dev spoke quietly. "You are ill as well. Let go."

"You don't believe in magic, Dev, do you? This—" He looked at his hands and shook them in the air, as if they tingled. "Is *not* magic. This is merely some infection, some illusion."

Dev stared at him. "It will make you dead, Matthais. Because it is something more than magic. Enough to be a science of its own. It is ghosts, chemicals, genetics, all of it combined. The valley is alive, its gems and its Jewels, and you cannot take them from here. You must beg forgiveness and let go."

Lurai thought of her grandmother, the way she'd spoken of the valley as something lost, something disappeared, something to still be protected. The way she'd leaned almost imperceptibly south, toward the fortress, when she did it. Lurai, too, felt that pull, toward the moonstone throne.

We are of the valley, Cousin.

She made up her mind then. Breaking herself from Matthais's grip, Lurai grabbed Dev, dodged the crumbling columns, and ran the last few steps to the throne. Together, the two of them placed the book on the seat and began to unwrap the last binding.

Doing so, Dev nicked her finger. A drop of the book's ink mixed with her blood.

That was supposed to be me, Lurai thought.

~

Dizzyingly, the entire room began to shake as the hum roared in Dev's ears. "Another quake?" Dev whispered. *Have we failed?* She turned to her colleagues. "You must take shelter," but they'd frozen. She was moving, but everyone else had slowed.

More. She could hear the Prince clearly now. And Lurai's

mother, Hanne, the former innkeeper. "Quickly, Lurai." Dev reached for the innkeeper's hand and felt the lapis shard there. Painfully slowly, Lurai made a small cut across her palm and pressed her hand against the book too.

The shaking continued. Dev realized it was her, not the palace, that was rocking: her cells being transformed. Just as she'd been warned. "I don't want this," she whispered, once, before her mouth turned to crystal and stopped her tongue.

The mineral taste filled her nostrils, made her eyes water: salt and stone. Anger. She tasted rage and want and so much yearning for power. So much capacity for it. It could be hers. All she had to do was take the throne for herself.

This belongs to the valley. I belong to the valley. With the last motion the gems coursing through her blood would allow, she pressed the book into the throne, unbound. At once, all the gem-taste receded. The gems poured from her blood into the book. They merged into the throne.

The humming ceased completely. Dev stepped back and helped Lurai seat herself on the throne. She closed her eyes.

Did we do the right thing? Dev wondered. *To trust the book? The valley? What if we've chosen wrong?*

When Lurai opened her eyes again, her irises had returned to their original hazel color. "I saw my mother," she whispered. Tears cascaded down her cheeks. But she didn't rise from her seat. "I promised to protect the gems and guide them. To protect the valley. I am the lapidary now, speaker of the new Jeweled Court."

Carefully, Dev knelt at her side. "And the Prince?"

"The Prince is with us. He attends the throne." Something about the new confidence in Lurai's voice made Dev believe, even as the rocking and pitching of the valley slowed.

"Dev," Vandina gasped. She pointed at Matthais's opal hands, dangling heavily at his sides. "You must help."

Dev showed them to Lurai.

Bring him forward. The writing on the floor before the throne began. A single letter looped toward Dev's foot. *But the others must stay far back.*

Lurai, the new lapidary, reached out for the academic in the half-sunken and dirt-filled moonstone court. Matthais winced as the opals dripped from his fingers, curling in letters and half words across the floor.

Matthais coughed, then whispered, "It hurts."

The throne—the moonstone throne—began to glitter with more gems, of all colors. Beyond the walls, too distant to make any sense to Dev's ears, she could hear shouting. Lurai dropped her hold on Matthais. Then the doors to the court swung open, and beyond them Dev saw the meadow, and the sky.

The palace of the Jeweled Court had risen once more.

The Prince and Lurai wrote and spoke as one.

The new court of the valley will emerge, and Lurai/I will lead it. Their words appeared on the court floor and on the columns as Dev and Vandina watched in shock. *The gems and the book and all the artifacts are ours. We have restored them.*

Somewhere not too far away, a pickaxe fell to the ground with a thud. Light poured into the court. Gemstones—both whole and shards—glittered, no longer hidden by the dust. A dig worker peered through the gap in the door.

Lurai turned toward the worker's shouts. *She can hear. She can move.*

Someone yelled for Lannert.

The Book of Gems, inscribed in silver now, and not in ruby or sapphire, rested on the throne. "It is done," Lurai said, her hand on it. Dev looked at her own hands, which were bare. The silver bindings had been stripped from them.

There would be no more words written by the book. Only the throne. Lurai lifted the lapis pages. They looked lighter now.

"This is no time for princes," Matthais whispered. His fingers were still tinted opal white. "The Six Republics will not listen to you."

"Then no one will share in the valley's true power," Lurai said, and the Prince wrote the words across the walls, the throne, the floor. "Our people, our history, our gems. We are willing to work with you. And also to ignore you and disappear, as we always have. We will no longer be your subjects."

Lannert called breathlessly from the doorway, "Perhaps it is time for the gems and the lapidaries, if not for a Prince!"

Dev stood and turned to the dig master. The quakes had lifted the throne room from the crevasse. The views from the windows showed people climbing the walls outside, peering in. And all around, valley diggers stared at Lurai, seated on the throne, then began to kneel.

"Dev, you were right all along," Matthais said as his hands regained their color, healed. "Not magic. Something more."

"Something very much more," Dev said. "The valley is alive. At once both human and gem."

The gems were as alive as the people who could hear them and speak for them. All that bound their power now was the valley itself. And a very strong young woman.

She had been well trained by her grandmother. Dev dropped to one knee, pulling Vandina and Matthais with her.

"I'm not sure this is best," Vandina said, but Dev shushed her.

"The valley requires manners." Dev honored her cousin. Lurai bent her head in acknowledgment.

"What would you have from us?" Lurai asked.

"Once, I would have asked for the gem-covered body of my former mentor, to throw into a crevasse," Dev admitted. "But I have resolved to never think of him again."

Lurai smiled. "You may rise. I wish you would stay. We need more gem-speakers. We will consider an appropriate reward."

For a moment, Dev thought of her grandmother's voice, her stories, her legacy. Then the scholar straightened her skirts and lifted her chin. "I have a talk to give, a Symposium," she said, finally. "About how none of this is magic. And how all of it is."

Then we will help you, Cousin, the gems wrote on the moonstone throne as Lurai spoke the words.

11.

THE SINGLE CARRIAGE, packed with everything Dev could fit in it, lumbered across the first bridge without falling to its demise.

More time, more time, the tracks clattered.

The second bridge wobbled, but the journey grew easier. Dev didn't clutch the armrest of the well-cushioned seat. She breathed easily, looking at the enameled ceiling of the elaborate Society car. Chairwoman Yance had personally sent it to pick her up in time for the Symposium.

And by the time they'd cleared the fourth bridge, Dev's mind had cleared too. She felt the wards on the bridge reacting to the gems that would always run through her blood. Gems that still begged her to return to the throne.

She refused, every day. Her resolve grew firmer each time she repeated the words: "I will speak of you, but not for you." The throne belonged to her cousin Lurai. Calia would inherit the Deaf King Inn. And Devina Brunai intended to be something else: a colleague.

Vandina and Matthais rode beside her, and Netherby's escritoire, mostly intact and working, skillfully repaired by Dev herself, fit in the box below her feet. It was evidence enough, she hoped.

Dev was bringing home proof. Of what, she could no longer be sure.

The valley's history had risen to meet its future. Although Chairwoman Yance did not yet know it, Dev traveled to the Symposium with that news, and all the proof the Prince and Lurai would allow them. Data, measurements, and more.

History. Ghosts. The past, living on, in every descendant of the valley, and every stone.

She knew now that the Society would welcome her. The carriage had arrived ahead of their departure, bearing a handwritten letter from Yance herself, apologizing profusely for not believing in her.

What Dev hadn't yet decided was whether she would meet them with a matching spirit of welcome.

When she fully understood what the Society's constant pursuit of knowledge had done to the valley she was reluctant.

But she had a task to accomplish and a message to deliver. She'd have plenty of time to decide what to do afterward.

Somewhere behind her, a new kingdom was rising from the valley, with an ancient prince and a fierce young woman on the throne.

And for that, the world needed to be ready.

Tick tick tick, Netherby's escritoire clamored, and she looked at the printout before showing it to the others. *You are free of your obligations once you pass the last bridge, Cousin.*

The message was unsigned. But it seemed to glitter in the light.

Dev responded to the Jeweled Valley, her fingers pressing the escritoire's keys gently: *I will remember anyway. And make sure others never forget.*

Acknowledgments

So many thanks to everyone at Tordotcom, especially Matt Rusin, Irene Gallo, Lee Harris, Christine Foltzer, Megan Kiddoo, Barbara Wild, and Lauren Hougen for giving this book its proper setting and polish. To Irene, Lee, Tommy Arnold, and Patrick Nielsen Hayden, with gratitude for your vision for each Gemworld book, and all of them together.

To Paul Race and to Chris Wagner, who let me mess about with metals, stones, and oxygen-acetylene torches. To Tom Wilde, who won't let me have an oxygen-acetylene torch in the house, but who answers any chemistry question put to him and only then asks, "Why do you want to know?"

To my agent, Andrea Somberg, and to Malka Older, E. Catherine Tobler, Scott Andrews, Julia Rios, Rachel Hartman, Elizabeth Bear, C. L. Polk, Sarah Monette, Kelly Lagor, Lauren Teffeau, Sarah Mueller, Chrises East and Gerwel, Curtis Chen, Siobhan Carroll, A. C. Wise, A. T. Greenblatt, Susan and Chris Lake, and Stephanie Feldman, who saw the facets of this story and in the Gemworld, even when it was rough. To my colleagues and students at Western Colorado University and VCFA.

To all of us who are making it through these times, together.

About the Author

Author photograph by Brian Djerballa

Fran Wilde's novels and short stories have been finalists for six Nebula Awards, a World Fantasy Award, four Hugo Awards, four Locus Awards, and a Lodestar Award. They include her Nebula and Compton Crook Award–winning debut novel, *Updraft,* and her Nebula Award–winning, Best of NPR 2019, debut middle-grade novel, *Riverland.* Her short stories have appeared in *Asimov's Science Fiction, Tor.com, Beneath Ceaseless Skies, Shimmer, Nature, Uncanny,* and multiple year's best anthologies.

Wilde teaches for Vermont College of Fine Arts' MFA in Writing for Children & Young Adults and the genre fiction MFA concentration at Western Colorado University, and also writes nonfiction for publications including *The Washington Post, The New York Times,* and *Tor.com.* You can find her on Twitter, Instagram, Facebook, and at franwilde.net.

TOR·COM

**Science fiction. Fantasy. The universe.
And related subjects.**

*

More than just a publisher's website, *Tor.com*
is a venue for **original fiction, comics,** and
discussion of the entire field of SF and fantasy,
in all media and from all sources. Visit our site
today—and join the conversation yourself.